The Thief
and Other Stories

Georg Heym

The Thief

and Other Stories

translated by Susan Bennett

Libris

The Thief and Other Stories first published as
Der Dieb. Ein Novellenbuch,
Ernst Rowohlt Verlag, Leipzig, 1913 ('Der Dieb', 'Der fünfte Oktober',
'Der Irre', 'Die Sektion', 'Jonathan', 'Das Schiff', 'Ein Nachmittag')

This English translation first published by Libris, 1994

Libris
10 Burghley Road
London NW5 1UE

A catalogue record for this book is available from the British Library

ISBN 1 870352 68 8

Designed and produced by Kitzinger, London
Printed and bound by Biddles Ltd, Guildford

Contents

The Thief

Aux sots je préfère les fous,
Dont je suis, chose, hélas! certaine.
                    Baudelaire

'God, I swear to Thee I will do Thy will. For Thou art the Lord, O Lord, and I am Thine Instrument through and through, now until eternity. Amen. That is to say: yes, yes, it must be done. I have prayed to Thee on my knees; Thou knowest it, night after night in the Gethsemane of this attic. If it be possible, Lord, take away this cup from me. Nevertheless, not what I will but what Thou wilt. And now I will gird myself and go out, as once Elijah did against the false priests, or Moses, when he strode out to confront the circling dancers. Not one more of these nights, Lord, or Thou wilt destroy my reason, and I need it, for Thou hast laid a great work upon my shoulders.'

He fell down before the Angel of the Lord, who stood behind the stove, there where his overcoat hung, which was the place where he always appeared recently.

Then he stood up, took the parcel, and went.

He did not know how it had begun. For a few years now he had withdrawn from his friends in an attack of sudden disgust. He was soon forgotten. His friends now knew nothing of his life. If one of them met him in passing he did not recognize him.

He had passed his time in all kinds of studies, trying to heal his tormenting melancholia. He became, successively, a biologist, an astronomer, an archaeologist, dropping each study in turn when it failed to satisfy him. All they had done was to fill him with even greater emptiness. And now he lived in a big boarding-house, buried in his little mansard room, lonely, unknown to anybody, one among the many lonely people of this great city.

He spent the evenings in the depths of his armchair watching the fading light and the cloud-ships of summer with their rosy keels travelling westwards, towards new, mysterious lands. Or in late summer when the days of the north-west wind begin, filling the sky with great strange images, he watched the heavenly animals which autumn drives out onto the green pastures: great whales, giant dromedaries, shoals of innumerable tiny fishes, disappearing over the oceans of heaven in the endless blue.

He made notes on all these remarkable apparitions. For instance once he saw the devil, against a wine-red background, straddling a heap of black bodies prostrated before him in prayer; then on another occasion he saw a monstrous bat, apparently pinned to the sky by its outstretched wings, as farmers nail bats to barn-doors; then there was a giant three-masted ship, trees on mountains, mighty lions, monstrous snakes laid around the shoulders of the sky, a giant monk with a dragging cassock, men with curious elongated profiles, and once a fiery angel who mounted the steps of the aether with a great torch.

Sometimes everything was filled with a strange almost inaudible music, like the roaring of the ocean in the darkness of unfathomable caves and underground domes.

The clouds were his last study, the last temptation, the most dangerous work of the devil.

One evening, he burnt the notebook, and from then on when he heard the storm driving the cloudy purple bucentaur over the horizon, he closed the shutters, sealed them with black cloths on the inside, and immersed himself entirely in darkness and silence.

That was when the voices began; over in a distant corner. They sounded as if coming up out of pipes, muffled and tired like the complaints of the dead floating around in the arteries of the earth.

He had not understood them in the first weeks, but gradually he learned their language as they gained power over him. And after he had fasted four days and watched four nights, he was granted the first vision, and experienced for the first time that feeling of endless bliss and immeasurable pain.

Slowly, like Christ who dwelt two years amid the horrors of the wilderness, he was prepared for his great journey. What sufferings, what fears, what sleepless nights, but also what hopes, what ecstasies, what visions! After his body had cast off the flesh, and the last remnants of animal matter had been purged from his blood, he learned one night of his mission, from a voice that rose over the sea like a clap of thunder.

Yes, woman was the original evil. Christ's work had been in vain. For how could he have saved the human race if it was always, of necessity, going to fall back into sin, as a stone falls back, though it be hurled as high as the clouds. Of a truth men were like poor flies trying to get out of a honey pot; they clambered and scrabbled but did not get far; they always had to go back down into sin; into the sweetness. And he read aloud from St Mark, Chapter 15, verse 34:

'And at the ninth hour Jesus cried with a loud voice, saying Eloi, Eloi, lama sabachthani? which is, being interpreted, My God, my God, why hast Thou forsaken me?'

Verse 37: 'And Jesus cried with a loud voice, and gave up the ghost'!

'My God, my God, why hast Thou forsaken me?' So that was the last word of Christ, and with it he buried his whole glory. In the horror of death he recognized the last truth. His work had been in vain: his entry into Jerusalem, the bloody scourging, the suffering, the way of the cross, the long hours on the dark tree. God had forsaken him, and his work had been in vain.

And the darkening of the heavens, the rending of the temple veil, the rising of the dead from their graves, were nothing but the shabby props of a bad and senseless play.

Yes, and he 'cried with a loud voice and gave up the ghost'.

And he continued reading, from the 17th chapter of the Revelation of St John the Divine:

'1. And there came one of the seven angels which had the seven vials, and talked with me, saying unto me, Come hither; I will shew unto thee the judgement of the great whore that sitteth upon many waters.

'2. With whom the kings of the earth have committed fornication, and the inhabitants of the earth have been made drunk with the wine of her fornication.

'3. So he carried me away in the spirit into the wilderness: and I saw a woman sit upon a scarlet coloured beast, full of names of blasphemy, having seven heads and ten horns.

'4. And the woman was arrayed in purple and scarlet colour, and decked with gold and precious stones and pearls, having a golden cup in her hand full of abominations and filthiness of her fornication . . .

'8. The beast that thou sawest was, and is not; and shall ascend out of the bottomless pit, and go into perdition: and they that dwell on the earth shall wonder, whose names were not written in the book of life from the foundation of the world, when they behold the beast that was, and is not, and yet is.'

'The beast that was, and is not, and yet is.'

And the profundity of these words shocked him.

He saw before him the neck of the devilish beast in its terrible sadness, with *the face of the woman* hanging over its horns, over her forehead the seal of death, and round her

5

mouth a terrible and heart-breaking smile, like the reflection of the hellish abyss.

So everything must be done again, for the beast was
not yet conquered.

The evil must be grasped at the root.

Adam was good as long as he was alone, but when
Satan wormed his way into the dream of God and told
him to create Woman, the moment of sin was implanted
in the future of the sexes. Whether man must fall
through the first woman, or later, through her daugh-
ters, was not determined; that he must fall was certain.

And the Messiah had done nothing about woman. That
was why God had forsaken him in the last hour.

There was a symbol. The women were always gathering around it, or passing by to suck in renewed strength
from it, like snakes which sometimes return into their
mysterious cities underground to fetch new poisons for
themselves.

And this symbol hung here, down the road two streets
along, in its own temple, and everything else that was
hanging round it was only there in order to conceal the
sign and keep the secret from the men. Yes, yes, that was
why the women all laughed so much when they gave in
their umbrellas in the cloakroom. God himself had told
him.

The first time he visited her was in the afternoon
hours, when she was surrounded by the crowds desiring
to sacrifice their hearts on the altar of the she-devil. So
she was less able to watch him, and did not immediately

recognize him as her enemy. In this way he was able to accustom himself gradually to her eyes. Every day he stayed a little longer, every day he grew more patient and strengthened himself more for the last fight with the dragon, like Mithridates who took stronger doses of poison every day to inure his blood to it.

In the beginning he used all the many precautions against the evil eye; on going into the room he would put the thumb of his left hand between the first two fingers, or he would carry a silver phallus on his person. But gradually he was able to do without them, and look into the eyes of the woman without peril.

And one day she noticed who was before her. There was a sudden movement across her face like a white shadow of recognition. She turned aside for an instant, then she joined battle with him. She looked through all the people, right at him in his corner. Their eyes met in the intervening space, like crossed daggers, or like two gulfs of an empty universe seeking to swallow each other up. Which will devour the other, which eternity will be greater, and engulf its opponent?

The victor here would have won the last battle, the enemy would be no more. Around the victor there would either be the measureless brightness of light, and the chorales of the suns, or a black sky full of desolate silence, and standing upon heaps of coffins, the black throne of Belial and the giant banners of hell.

And so in the crowded room he fought the first battle, the first wordless struggle. No one saw him, no one took any notice of him, no one admired him. Not one of these miserable fools knew what events, what deeds were taking place here, they had no idea what destinies were at stake on this terrible bloodless battlefield. If he had had time in the midst of the strife, he would have driven them all out of the temple, these usurers and idolaters. But he dared not divert his attention.

His eyes began to hurt; he saw the woman through a red fire, he felt on the point of collapse. He had to sit down on a chair, but he held out.

And he began to feel that he was winning. Her eyes were no longer so hard, so large, so confident of victory. Something like a shadow passed over her forehead, and he saw that she was growing tired, and slowly letting go. She seemed to be disappearing from the foreground, her outline grew shadowy, her face grew smaller. And it seemed to him that she was sinking back into the mysterious landscape behind her as though into a veil of green, still water.

And suddenly she was only the ordinary Mona Lisa Gioconda, which droves of English and Americans were herded past every day like swine.

The first battle of the heavenly war was won. He collapsed into a chair.

Later, when he was leaving, he turned towards her once more from the door. Their eyes met a last time, and he caught a look which was meant to be ironic, but only thinly covered the oceans of rage beneath. And once more he mastered her, and scared her back into her rocky desert. As he went through the door, he knew that she was watching him, and he felt as if an assassin were standing behind his back. But he did not strike home; he had lost his nerve.

He was outside, in the brilliance of the streets, and he had to keep a hold on himself or he would have danced and sung, and shouted his happiness up at the dawning heat of the sky.

In the afternoon he had an amusing time leaning far out of the window and watching the people down below. He ate a bag of plums, and dropped the stones on the tiny people's heads. 'If they only knew,' he thought, 'damned philistines, if those idiots only knew!' and his big bristling beard was shaken by a loud laugh.

From then on he began to visit his female foe at other times, when it was empty in the Louvre, towards evening, when the pictures awaken from the sleep of the day. In those mysterious hours when the light is going out of the afternoon, in the half darkness of the deserted rooms, every head becomes deeper and stranger in the prison of its frame.

He had got into the habit of eavesdropping on her from a distance while she believed herself unobserved, before stepping out in front of her.

She was never so beautiful as when the fires of the sinking sun lay shimmering in the dust of the room upon her forehead, and her dark hair began to gleam as if with its own light. Then she seemed to grow forward out of the dark background, to become flesh, and to bask in the light of her own shamelessness. Perhaps that was precisely the hour in which the soul of the depraved artist had opened itself to the devil and conceived her. For her face sometimes looked as though she were remembering a remote, distant hour full of secret lust.

Oh, yes, anyone else would have been taken in by her, and sometimes he too might have weakened, but then he called in spirit on the Lord, and the Lord filled his heart with hate and with divine rage.

Then he stepped forward. He felt how she started and went cold with fear, saw loathing for him gathering on her forehead. And then the struggle began again, day after day, without sound, without words. Sometimes he believed he had got her to the point where she no longer dared take up the fight. She hung in her frame like an ordinary picture; her eyes were without light; she was enveloped in a vapour of melancholy and remorse. Then he felt sorry for her and tormented her no longer. He saw her with the eyes of a doctor coming to rescue her. He would have to make a large incision – undoubtedly a kill-or-cure operation. She would have to be blinded. But if she succumbed then perhaps she would find mercy with God. She must at least be brought to repentance, for 'joy shall be in heaven over one sinner that repenteth, more than over ninety and nine just persons, which need no repentance'.

But suddenly there she was laughing again, and he could not help but see she had only been mocking him, and that it had all been an insolent pretence.

The guards no longer took any notice of him.

They joked about the madman, but apart from that did not particularly concern themselves with him. He always greeted them very politely, and every so often he gave them a handsome tip if he wanted to stay on longer than the rules permitted. Then one of the porters would let him out by a back door.

In August there were several suicides of young people, all of which the newspapers attributed to disappointed love. Evidently God must have read about them, for He responded by stepping up the pace of His intervention.

The angel who customarily transmitted the heavenly messages had been hinting for some days that the hour for the deed was near, and today he told him that the divine Council had settled upon the 17 August.

He had not been there for a whole day, in order to make her uneasy and confuse her by an abrupt change of routine. It was a clever tactic on his part – or so he kept telling himself. Actually it was fear that had come over him; suddenly, after the angel had brought the message. He had run out of the house, to be among people, to hide himself from God. But God was after him. He saw Him everywhere: in between the omnibuses, among the people. Wherever he ran, he met the number 17: on the doorplates of houses, on the trams. The very number that he would most like to have erased. He was certain, whenever he raised his eyes, that he would see a 17 and he saw one.

He heard a snatch of conversation behind him: 'When

the trumpeter steps out from the gate.' 'But that's tomorrow.' 'Oh yes, of course, tomorrow is the 17th.'

That decided it. The heavenly Father was sending His policemen out after him everywhere; he would never be able to get away from Him. He remembered the words: 'And if I came to the farthest sea, You would still be there.' Yes, no one could hide from the face of God, even by creeping into the fiery throat of Satan.

That remark about the trumpet was clearly an allusion to the Last Judgement and the punishment awaiting him if he disobeyed. And he turned around and gave himself up to his destiny.

Afternoon, night, and morning he passed in prayer. He lay before God in the dust; he humbled himself; he tore his whole soul apart and let God stream in like smoke, like an aura. About midnight his lamp went out. He continued to pray in the dark. And from the ends of his hands, which he was waving about in the darkness, there shone a faint blue light like St Elmo's fire, as if the strength of God was pouring into him like a river, to fill him with ecstasy.

He swelled with strength like a warrior; he could have hypnotized a whole city; he could have forced the midnight horizons to their black knees before him, and drawn the dark ocean behind him like a gigantic stormy mantle, if he had gone forth.

The more he submitted himself to God, the more fiery became his longing to pit himself against the princes of Hell; the Beelzebubs and the mighty Leviathans of the

12

abyss. Because naturally they too were making their preparations.

Perhaps hundreds of thousands of them were already lurking behind the picture; perhaps they had bored huge tunnels up through the enigmatic mountains behind the Goddess's back, and were sitting there clad in fiery armour, waiting to fall on him if he tried to touch the picture. Then the armies of hell would break out in a shrieking, stinking nocturnal holocaust, the cohorts of Satan coming to burn and devour him, the Louvre, Paris, France, the world, everything.

And perhaps tomorrow at this time chaos would reign once more: a sky would be without stars, and a great satiated dragon would dance on the tip of its tail over the flames.

And now the hour had come.

There was no longer any way back.

God had spoken.

He stood downstairs, at the door, and his knees were trembling so much, he was so little in control of his nerves, that he had to lean against the wall.

In order to think everything over once more, to calm himself, he decided to take a stroll first. So he tried wandering off into a couple of streets that were full of people. But he did not manage to merge into the crowd. By contrast with their profusion, their aimlessness, their transience, his greatness and loneliness stood out, like the fire of an eternal lamp or the footstep of a god wandering invisible through the streets. Many people stared at him. They seemed to be surprised by him. He had hidden his eyes behind large glasses, so as not to betray their brightness. His lips were moving in prayer. The frayed tails of his black coat flew out behind him, and at every step his large hat slipped further over his forehead. As he crossed a roadway, a policeman stared after him.

The battle was to begin down by the Seine, for Hell had placed its outposts far ahead. Boughs were being sawn off a tree and one of them fell directly onto his head. He looked up and saw the whole sky filled with demons, hundreds upon hundreds of them riding on red clouds, devils with great horns on their foreheads, others with trumpets. Mighty steeds reared into the sky, giant lances were swung, and a tremendous cry filled the north-western sky, far away over the roof of the Louvre and beyond. The blood left his face. Despite the afternoon heat, a dreadful feeling of cold came over his body. His veins were like shrivelled roots, and his brain spun like a top in the narrow confines of his skull.

In his fear he began to pray aloud. Some children who had been playing in the street ran after him. He made an effort to regain his self-control, and went up to a soft drinks stall for a lemonade. Then he started on his way again, quite calm and composed. The children wandered off.

That was his last fit of weakness. From then on, God was with him.

He entered the Louvre with his parcel under his arm.

14

The porter greeted him; he gave him a tip. Upstairs in the galleries it was already empty, and the oppressive silence of all the pictures in the twilit rooms was like that of people who have been talking about someone. He came in and they suddenly went dumb. But the malicious conversations of these lesser devils, these shadows and dead people, still seemed to be vibrating in the room, and to carry on reverberating in his ears.

An attendant was sleeping on a chair in the dusk. When he heard footsteps he awoke. He looked at his watch: it was closing-time.

The madman went up to him, gave him a five-franc piece and said he should come and fetch him in two hours and let him out. The guard took the tip and went away, yawning loudly.

Now he was quite alone: a lonely man on the remotest foothills of life, with the terror of the last, invisible secrets. All the dead eyes of the people from bygone centuries stared haughtily down at him from the darkness of their frames as he passed by them. And there was a continuous rustling and whispering behind his back, as if they were only waiting for him to have gone by before making fun of him. In every corner someone seemed to be waiting for him, a big, dark presence, which moved on each time he advanced towards it. He heard footsteps behind him; what was that? He stopped; they stopped. He went on; they began again. Suddenly he realized it was only the distant echo of his own footfall.

It was growing darker; a storm seemed to be blowing

up in the sky. A mighty roaring filled the air outside. A mass of leaves and dust blew across one of the windows, high up. Somewhere in the galleries, a rustling sound started; the wind must have found a way in somewhere; it sounded like whimpering, and the blood froze in his veins with horror.

Behind the entrance to the Gioconda's room there was a large armchair. He let himself down on his hands, and crept on all fours like an animal through the antechamber, then quickly through the door, and concealed himself behind the broad back of the chair.

He had lost all his courage; fear shook him hither and thither in its giant fist. He would very much rather have turned back. But if he was weak now the devils would certainly jump on him and wring his neck in two seconds. He would lie there, like an empty sack, and humanity would have to wait another few thousand years for its redemption. He tried to think, he wanted to prise himself from the fingers of terror. He made a great effort to regain his self-control, tried to think about something neutral. He counted the strands of the fringe on the armchair, he began to pray, and at last, as no one came, his agitation began to abate. 'Thy will be done,' he murmured once more, and then stuck his head out cautiously from behind the chair.

And there she hung.

She saw him, she remained calm, she did not even start. Evidently she must have been forewarned, perhaps she had even seen him creeping in.

In the darkness of the densely-clouded sky her face seemed to shine with a triple light of mendacity and malice. Whatever gave her that angry look? There was hardly a line on her face. But it was more fearful to see than if it had been striated with wrinkles of fury. And suddenly he was able to view her quite calmly. He studied and scrutinized her, from the pure forehead, which seemed lit by a halo, down to the hands which were versed in all the vicious arts of fornication, in treachery, in dagger-play and the mixing of innocent white poisons. He interrogated her face. He wanted to find out where the real site of her baseness was, but he got no answer. He rose up behind his chair and waited. It seemed as though her lips were trembling with softly-spoken words, like butterflies over an evening meadow.

Ah! She was so beautiful in her depravity!

Was she silent, or was she speaking? Oh, he could have wished he had better ears, to learn all her basenesses, so that he could be doubly justified in damning her.

What wisdom of the abyss, what thoughts from hell might live behind her forehead? Into what depths might one have looked, if one could have forced open the silver portal of those temples? Ah, God!

In the silence he heard the blood roaring in his head; it sounded like an underground stream rushing past his ears in the spacious silence of these rooms, where words from her lips were perhaps still shimmering away into stillness, like drops that have fallen into a silver basin.

A shadow slid over her face like mourning. Her mouth seemed to shut, and she was silent.

But the silence which emanated from her was like an eternal song, like the roaring of distant, blue, unfathomable seas.

The storm outside was over. Only the occasional gust of wind still shook the tallest trees. The evening sun threw a blazing torch inside, and the deep Lombard colours of the portrait came to life in vivid purple. Her gown burst into a rush of flame and the red light spread up over her face and was caught in the golden net of her quiet laughter. And gradually she appeared to dissolve into the dusk, like a perfume, like a breath: the mountains behind her, her forehead, her hair, everything was on the point of dissolving into blue shadow. Only her smile remained bathed in light, soft like the silvery sound of an infernal harp, her smile like the deep golden reflection of the kisses of Ariman, the great seal of Satan, which he had branded on her lips in the fire of his embrace.

And now she must perish. Yes, it must be; those were his orders. And, when all was said and done, he could not defy God. For God had no one else but him.

She must be destroyed. Yes, oh yes, she was very beautiful. But it was all to no avail; her hour had come. And the last battle must begin.

He turned around, kneeled on the ground, got out his Bible and read the words of the Apocalypse once more:

'I saw a woman sit upon a scarlet coloured beast, full of names of blasphemy, having seven heads and ten horns.

And the woman was arrayed in purple and scarlet colour, and decked with gold and precious stones and pearls, having a golden cup in her hand full of abominations and filthiness of her fornication.'

Yes, full of abominations . . .

His hairy grey mane had fallen over his face, his glasses had slipped down over his grey nose, and as he knelt there he looked like a very aged ape squatting over his food at the end of his murky den.

And he continued reading, from the Epistle to the Hebrews, Chapter 6, Verse 4:

'For it is impossible for those who were once enlightened, and have tasted of the heavenly gift, and were made partakers of the Holy Ghost,

And have tasted the good word of God, and the powers of the world to come,

If they shall fall away, to renew them again unto repentance; seeing they crucify to themselves the Son of God afresh, and put him to an open shame.'

Yes, if he were to defect, if he, who had seen the heavens standing open, were to revoke his obedience to God, then he would be putting himself to open shame, crucifying himself, the true Messiah and messenger of God. And then he would be consigned to the deepest pit, in the bowels of hell. So there was no choice anyway.

He hid the book, stood up, went once more through all the rooms; everywhere was empty.

He went back, placed himself once more behind his chair, and once more gathered together all his strength.

Would he conquer, or would he be torn apart? Yet he was calm, his fear had gone. She could fall on him and tear him apart for all he cared. He bowed himself down before God one more time as he passed the upper window, committed his soul to Him, then went forward slowly, calling aloud to Heaven for help at every step.

He came near to the picture. No one moved. He looked all round him. Only over in one corner, where it was dark in the twilight, did he seem to see a swaying movement, like a giant formless shadow.

He still did not dare to touch her. But he stood in front of her, very close, and looked at her. He plunged his eyes into hers for the last battle. And she responded. Hell had take up the challenge.

And there they stood opposite each other, the madman and the woman, a tattered storm and an eternal stillness.

His face went as dark as a dying candle, but the woman's forehead seemed to be lit by the pale dawn of a timeless eternity. And whereas his face, even frozen as it was into a convulsive grimace, had a changing quality like a cloud-filled sky above a stormy sea, her face was like a spring, over which shadows and pictures are constantly passing, but whose water remains perpetually at rest.

Nothing happened. Nobody came. And time was passing. Something would have to be done soon, or it would be too late. He had to take the final step and seize her.

And the second after that the darkness might come, and the earth rise up, and the heavens cave in: night, wailing, fire and noise, and the ocean might rise like a raging storm and envelop the evening and put out the light of the stars. Perhaps their hands were over him already. He looked up furtively once more.

Then he waved the spread fingers of his left hand slowly in front of the picture, holding his right hand clenched in readiness for a fight.

He touched her hands; nothing moved. He held her head, nothing, nothing at all.

He touched her with his right hand, nobody moved, all was still, all was dark.

And now he seized the picture by the frame, lifted it off its hooks, laid it on the floor, wrapped it in the paper from the parcel that he had brought, so that now it looked just like the parcel. For a moment he leaned against the wall. Then he took the picture under his arm and went downstairs. The guard opened up for him; they wished each other good-evening, and he disappeared into the night.

Next morning all the newspapers knew about the theft of the Mona Lisa Gioconda.

All the guards were questioned immediately, but they naturally avoided giving away their own carelessness. They simply hadn't seen anything; didn't know anything.

Hundreds of statements were taken; crowds of unfortunate tramps were swept up off all the country roads of

France and submitted to minute cross-examination. Huge swarms of detectives took up position on every ocean steamer, a hundred thousand policemen raced after a hundred thousand different clues. All the murderers and thieves had a wonderful time, and all the art historians began making money at a furious pace. The whole of Paris got into a wild uproar, and every suburban shopkeeper had to have a picture of the Mona Lisa over his bed.

A spring night in Florence. A soft light shimmered low in the sky like the coming of dawn, over the dark, round, Etrurian mountains. And then the moon rose from behind them.

Suddenly all the streets leading down from the mountains lay in its white light, and all the roofs and towers of the city beneath the moon emerged from the night, vague and shapeless like the cities of a dream-kingdom. The silver squares of the river lay sparkling between the dark bridges.

He turned round, and a moonbeam hung in her eyes like a golden drop.

She could not be seen distinctly as the shadow of the curtain was moving across her face. Only a strip from her chin to her forehead was uncovered and shone in the moonlight. Perhaps she was crying?

Oh, if only she had cried, only a single drop, a single tear of repentance.

He tore the curtain away from the window before she had time to catch his movements. He had guessed right;

crying was the last thing she felt like doing. No thought of repentance dared show itself upon that sinful brow. She was as blooming as ever in her shamelessness; only death would wipe that look from her mouth.

She had got no better since he had imprisoned her here; she had got worse, the whore. Perhaps Satan had been with her every night, while he was fleeing through half the world to forget his love for her.

How many nights of tears, Oh, devil, Mona Lisa Gioconda, Oh, God.

When he had come to Florence he had rented this little house overlooking the city. And the very first night he had wanted to kill her. Yes, that was three years ago, when he was still strong. Oh yes, and now? All the people in the street laughed in his face.

At one time he had held his knife to her eyes, but he had not been able to strike. For a bitter recognition had made him weak; he suddenly knew that he loved her. Oh, my God, that was the most terrible thing, those desperate struggles that had begun at that time and gone on for weeks. Every night, when he had no need to fear her eyes, the point of his knife had been at her face, but each time he had let his arm fall, and had sat there in the corner, always in the same place, huddled together like a beaten dog, and had no longer dared to look at her.

One day he hid her here and shut her in. And then he was off, through who knows how many cities, chased by the whirlwind of his love round Florence, through Spain, Tunisia, Greece, away over the Alps, always in a circle like a small comet which cannot pull itself out of the orbit of a too-powerful sun.

Finally he could not carry on. God had forsaken him. And now he lay like a wreck thrown up onto a sandbank by the storm.

God had gone. Perhaps God had died and was buried somewhere in heaven. Quite different gods were perhaps sitting on His seat.

Now he wanted to make just one more experiment. He did not want a beloved who was attached to one person one day and another the next. If she would only stop being false, if she would stop laughing, he would sell himself to the devil on the spot, and sit for eternity in hell at her feet like a little demon, or a small winged butterfly hovering eternally over the gigantic gardens of her neck.

The moon came wholly into the room.

All the objects moved back and shrank in its blue light.

But the face of the Mona Lisa grew wide as a lake.

He went up to her and said: 'I will forgive you, I will love you, but you must not laugh any more.' And to allow her time to change her face he turned round.

He saw his Bible on a chair. He threw it out of the window and heard it land with a smack down below. Then he went to the window and stuck out his tongue at God.

When he turned back to her, things had not improved an atom. He decided to take stronger measures, because you couldn't show weakness towards a pigheaded woman.

And he suddenly realized that that laugh would be a blasphemy, an impossibility, on a man's face.

Oh, he despised her, but he loved her. And he despised himself for loving this whore who had known how to drag him, the holy one of God, down into the mud with her.

Well, none of that mattered now; he just loved her, and about that there was nothing more to be done.

But the laugh had to go, that accursed laughter was unbearable. And he began his incantation.

He sprang like a devil at the picture, three leaps forward, three leaps back, his arms flailing in the air, his crooked hands like two beaks above his head, and his long, neglected hair dancing on his thin shoulders. With every spring he bent his knees together and his big black shadow danced near him on the wall, three leaps forward, three leaps back, on and on like a giant kangaroo.

But it was all to no avail.

'So you won't,' he thought at last. 'But I'll make you sit up, you'll see. You think I'm your fool. Well, I'll show you.'

He lit the light in front of her and held it under her nose, just to tickle her a bit. Perhaps now she would finally cry out. And she did seem to screw up her face a bit, but only as if her lips were widening into a bigger grin, mocking his useless exertion even more.

And suddenly he threw the light away. 'What have I

done,' he thought, and he fell on his knees before her, and cried in front of her, so that his shoulders shook with sobs.

And suddenly he heard her laugh, quite loudly.

And no man can stand for that.

His whole love was gone. Suddenly he was like stone. He stood up, got the light out again and, shielding the little flame with his hand, went down the stairs. The reflected glow chased over his face which was red and stiff.

In the kitchen below he looked out a large knife, long and broad, the meat-cutting kind. And then he went upstairs again. As he stepped into the doorway of the attic room he held the candle up and let the glow play on her face.

Carefully, he looked for a place to begin. The eyes were the wickedest part, certainly. You could also of course go for the heart, kill her immediately, but that would not be revenge enough.

He stepped up to her and put the point of the knife to the inner corner of the right eye, stuck it in a little way and began to cut out the eye. It was not easy, as the old canvas was hard and stiff. Finally it only hung by a thread. He tore it out, and stamped it out with his foot while it was still trembling.

He did the same with the left eye, but that was even more firmly stuck, it didn't want to come out when he pulled it, and when he finally got it free a large shred of the forehead was left sticking to it.

But that was not quite the end. Now it was the turn of the mouth. He could not help stroking it one more time, running his index finger just once more gently over those lips.

Then, he struck: in the right-hand corner of the mouth where the smile was at its most wicked.

He continued cutting above and below till he got to the middle of the mouth then lifted out a little piece. Then he took a few steps back and contemplated his work like an artist. He did not trouble to do any more cutting, but grabbed the bit that was hanging loose in his clenched fist and tore it out, right across the face, holding his belly with laughter.

It was frightful to look at, this head, which death had suddenly broken out of from the inside like a prisoner out of his hole. The head with the uncanny eye-sockets, like windows with darkness behind them. And this big empty mouth, which really was no longer smiling now, but had drawn apart into the frightful grimace of death, an inaudible laugh which could yet be heard, which could not be seen and yet was there, ancient and dark as the centuries.

And suddenly, as he surveyed his work, he could see the essence of things, and he knew that there was nothing, no life, no being, no world, nothing, only a great black shadow all around him. And he was quite alone, up above on a rock. And he had only to take a single step and he would sink down into the eternal abyss.

A fearful tiredness came over him. And of course there

was nothing left to do. He went and crouched in a corner under an attic-window, like a black animal in the square of blue moonlight.

He had gone to sleep. And as he sat there leaning against the wall, his head hanging down between his knees and his long arms limp on the ground, as though they were about to trickle away from him, he resembled a big black caved-in heap of ashes from which the last glow has gone.

The light which he had thrown away had fallen on some rags, which gradually began to smoulder. It took a little while, but eventually the spark had nibbled its way over to a heap of straw. A wind came in and a little red fire-snake coiled up out of the dry stalks.

After another little while a few lost drunks who were wandering in the street saw something like a great red fiery dragon sitting on the roof and beating the burning rafters with its gigantic wings.

Events took their course. The drunks began to yell, a few windows opened, a few nightcaps nodded outside, a few house-doors opened, and three or four figures ran down the street towards the yellow lamp of the police-station.

The street fills up with people, with quarrelling and noise, children's screams and police; everyone stares up at the fire. A burning beam detaches itself and falls to the ground with a crash. More shrieking. A few people — wounded or dead — are taken away.

The fire service arrives, hoses spout into the fire, and a

great cloud of yellow steam ascends into the night as the jets pound the flames. A great ladder turns in the air like a crane, high up, where the head of the old man is leaning out of the attic window.

The ladder comes to rest leaning against the wall and a few firemen with big helmets run up the rungs like apes. When they are nearly at the top, the head goes back in. The watchers see them leaping through the glowing rafters after a black shadow which flees before them, in and out between the blaze and the beams, like two great devils chasing a mouse. Then the wild chase disappears abruptly rearwards in a cloud of smoke.

When the firemen found the old man in his corner at the back, through the fire and smoke, he was cowering over a bundle of things. He was holding something large in front of his face, a painting without eyes and mouth, but his eyes were looking at them through the holes in the mask, large and wild, and his long tongue was wagging out of the picture's empty mouth.

They tried to take the picture away from him: he held fast onto it. They tried to carry him out with the picture: he kicked them in the belly.

Half the roof fell in with a crash; the men were already close to suffocation. They tried once more to drag him out, but the old man let go of the picture with one hand, pulled out a blazing roof-beam with great glowing nails from above his head, and hit one of the fireman in the face with it so that he fell in a heap.

Then the other two were struck with horror, and they

left the dead man and the injured man lying where they were, and tried to get back outside where there was air. They sprang into the smoke as it billowed fiercely towards them, but they could no longer find the way; they threw away their helmets to see better, they ran back again on the other side past the old man, jumping over fiery ruins, then back the other way, past the old man again, and as they flew past him, even in their despair they heard his loud laughter ringing behind them.

The flames seized them. They struck at them with their bare hands, running, beating, and suddenly they were two blazing pillars of fire; they ran back again but there was a burning wooden wall, they ran to the right, and there was a stone wall; they could go no further, they screamed and beat against the stones with their roasting hands, nothing, nothing, the fire ate their hair, their skulls, the flames rent their eyes, they were blind, they saw nothing, the fire ate their faces, the flesh flew in pieces from their hands, but still in death they hammered the charred stumps of their fists against the wall.

The Fifth of October

On the fifth of October the bread-carts from Provence were supposed to come to Paris. The City Council had posted the news on all the street corners in its usual bold red lettering. And the people milled around in front of the notices all day as though waiting for the doors to open on some new and startling revelation. Starved to the bone, they dreamed of heavenly states of repletion, of monstrous wheat buns and floury white pies sizzling in every kitchen.

There'll be smoke from every chimney. We'll string up the bakers from the street lamps. We'll cook for ourselves, sink our arms elbow-deep in flour. The white stuff will cover the streets like fruitful snow, the wind will blow it like a thick cloud across the sun.

On every street great tables will be set up. Paris will hold a great communal feast, a mighty sabbath.

The people crowded in front of the locked cellars of the bakers' shops and squinted down at the empty kneading-troughs behind the iron-barred windows. They gloated at the black mouths of the giant fireless ovens, waiting hungrily, like them, for bread.

On one street of a quartier in Mont Parnasse a baker's shop was broken into, more out of boredom and to pass the time than in the hope of finding any bread in the bins.

Three men, coal-heavers from St Antoine, brought out the baker. They threw off his wig and stood him under the crooked lamp at his door. One pulled off the waistband of his trousers, wound it into a noose and threw it round his neck. Then he stuck his black fist in his face and shouted: 'You damned mealworm, now we're going to string you up.'

The baker began to wail, and looked round the bystanders for support, but all he saw was grinning faces.

Jacobus the shoemaker stepped forward and said to the men from the suburbs: 'Gentlemen, we'll let the swine go, but first he must repeat a prayer after me.'

'Yes, repeat a prayer,' whimpered the baker. 'Let me repeat a prayer.'

Jacobus began, 'I'm the God-damned swine of a baker.'

The baker repeated, 'I'm the God-damned swine of a baker.'

Jacobus: 'I'm a filthy Jew of a flour-hoarder. I stink a mile off.'

The baker: 'I'm a filthy Jew of a flour-hoarder. I stink a mile off.'

Jacobus: 'I pray to the Holy Saints every day that no one will notice all the rubbish I put in the bread.'

The baker repeated that as well.

The audience brayed. An old woman sat down on the steps and cackled like an old hen laying an egg.

Jacobus himself was laughing too much to go on.

For a while the comic anathema continued, but at last the people got tired of their wretched Aunt Sally and left him standing there with his noose still round his neck.

It began raining hard, and the people stepped under the roofs. The baker was gone. Only his white wig still lay in the middle of the square, coming apart in the rain. A dog got it in his mouth and dragged it away.

Gradually the rain abated and the people stepped out again onto the street. Hunger began gnawing at them again. A child had convulsions and the bystanders looked on and gave good advice.

Then suddenly the word went round: 'The bread carts are here! The bread carts are here!' The cry flew from one end of the street to the other. And the whole street began crowding out of the city gates. They came to the country, into the bare fields; they saw a deserted sky and long rows of poplars down the highroad, disappearing over the bleak horizon of the plain. Overhead, a flock of ravens flew before the wind towards the towns.

The human streams poured into the fields. Some had empty sacks on their shoulders, others had pots, or butcher's carrying-troughs, to take the bread away in.

And they waited for the carts, searching the rim of heaven like a tribe of astronomers looking for a new constellation.

They waited and waited, but they saw nothing but the cloudy sky and the storm bending the tall trees this way and that.

From a church, midday chimed slowly into the silent

crowds. Then they began to recall that at this hour in times gone by they had sat round a full table with a great white loaf resplendent in the middle like a stout king. And the word 'bread' thrust itself in their brain, in all its whiteness, all its fatness, and lay there like a stone in the sun: massive, crisp, ready to cut. They closed their eyelids and felt the juice of the wheat dripping over their hands. They felt the warmth of the holy clouds from the bread ovens, a rosy flame in which the white loaves toasted till their crusts were black.

And their hands trembled with longing for the flour. They shivered with hunger, and their tongues began chewing in their empty mouths, they swallowed air, and their teeth snapped involuntarily, as if they were crushing mouthfuls of white bread.

Some hung handkerchiefs out of their mouths, and their big teeth gnawed around them slowly, like machines. They had closed their sunken eyes and were rocking their heads as they sucked their dummies, in time to a secret, tormenting music.

Others sat on the kerbstones and cried with hunger, while big dogs, so thin their bones almost stuck through their hair, hung around their knees.

A fearful tiredness came over the motionless crowds. A monstrous paralysing apathy fell like a heavy blanket over their white faces.

Oh, their willpower was gone, stifled by hunger in a slow process of emasculation which sunk them in a terrible sleep full of tormenting dreams.

The plains of France sloped far and away around them, surrounded by ghostly mills which ringed the horizon like towers or giant corn-gods, stirring up clouds of flour with their arm-like sails, as if incense were smoking about their great heads.

Monstrous tables stood at the borders of France, swaying under the weight of huge bowls. Someone was beckoning the crowds forward. But they were tied to beds of torture; the terrible opium of hunger had numbed their blood, congealing it to a black mass of cinders. They wanted to cry out: 'Bread, bread, only a mouthful! Pity, mercy, only a mouthful, dear God.' But they could not open their lips; it was frightful: they were dumb. Frightful: they could not move a limb. They were crippled.

And black dreams fluttered over the clumps of sitting and lying people: an army condemned to eternal death, struck dumb for ever; condemned to sink back into the belly of Paris, to suffer, to be hungry, to be born and die in a sea of darkness, of secret conspiracies, of hunger and slavery, oppressed by bloodsucking tax-farmers, worn out by the endless drain on their strength, unmanned by the eternal miasma of the alleys, withering like an old parchment in the biting air of their miserable caves, condemned one day to stiffen in death in a dirty bed, a curse on their lips for the priest who came in the name of his God, the state, and authority, to reward their patience in a life of suffering by wringing out their last penny as a legacy to the church.

The sun never shone into their graves. What did they know of sun, in their ghastly dens? They saw it sometimes for an hour or so at midday, floating over the city, deadened by its exhalations, veiled in thick clouds. Then it disappeared. The shadows re-emerged from under the houses and the octopus arms of the alleys crept up them with their cold embrace.

How often they had stood by the Luxembourg gardens and looked through the ranks of grenadiers at the broad sunny meadows. They had stared at the court ladies dancing, the gold-braided courtiers with their shepherds' crooks, the bowing moors, the salvers full of oranges, biscuits and sweetmeats, the Queen in her golden carriage driving slowly round the park, like a Syrian goddess, a monstrous Astarte, stiff with white silk and glittering like a saint with a thousand pearls.

Oh! how often they had drunk the spicy perfume of musk, been almost overcome by the sweet smell of ambergris drifting out of the park as from a mysterious temple. Oh! surely they could have been allowed inside just once, to sit on one of those velvet chairs, and drive in just such a carriage. They could quite happily have struck the whole National Assembly dead and kissed the King's feet, if for just one hour he had made them forget their hunger and the bare fields with their harvest of despair.

And they pressed their noses against the iron railings, and stuck their hands through the bars; crowds of beggars, herds of outcast and whimpering people. And their horrible smell drifted into the park, like a cloud during a gloomy sunset that precedes a terrible dawn. They clung onto the railings like gruesome spiders, and their eyes wandered far into the park, with its evening meadows, its hedges and laurel walks, and the marble statues which simpered down at them from their pedestals. Little gods of love, putti stout as fattened geese with arms like white overstuffed sausages, aimed their love-darts at the people's open mouths and waved at them with their stone quivers, while the bailiffs who had come to throw them in the debtors' prison clamped their heavy hands upon their shoulders.

The sleepers groaned and the others envied them their sleep.

They stared straight ahead, looking down the road for the bread-carts: a road rendered lifeless and desolate by the alarms of revolution, which like a dead intestine brought no more supplies into the belly of France. It was white and tailed off at the horizon into the pale brow of the unheeding sky, a sky as fat as a priest's face, as pudgy as a bishop's cheek, as unwrinkled as an overfed begging friar. It was as peaceful as a village Mass; it was gently framed by little afternoon clouds like an old abbé sleeping after lunch in his sacristy, coffined in an armchair with his curly wig drooping over his forehead.

The human herd's rags stank horribly. Their dirty scarves fluttered round their grey faces. Gusts of suppressed crying flitted through the terrible silence. As far as the eye could see, tattered three-cornered hats stuck into the air, some with dirty ostrich-feathers dancing upon them. The scattered figures resembled the frozen steps of a sombre minuet, a *danse macabre* petrified by the passage of Death into a great black heap of stones, transfixed by pain into pillars of silence. Uncountable Lots, melted down by the flames of a hellish Gomorrah into eternal rigidity.

High above them in the cold October sky went the iron plough of time, which furrowed his fields with suffering and sowed them with need, so that one day the flame of revenge might arise, so that one day the arms of these thousands might become light, light and carefree as soaring doves while the guillotine swung its reaper's knife, so that one day they might step out under heaven, like gods of the future, bare-headed in the eternal dawn of a never-ending Whitsuntide.

A black dot appeared on the whiteish sky at the far end of the highway.

The ones in front saw it and pointed it out to each other.

The sleepers awoke and sprang up. Everyone stared down the road. Was that black dot the Mecca they sought; was it their salvation?

For a few moments they all believed it was. They forced themselves to believe it.

But the dot grew too quickly. Now they could all see that this was not the slow progress of a host of carts, it was not a flour-caravan. And hope left their foreheads and disappeared into the wind.

But what was it? Who was riding so wildly? Who had a reason to ride like that in this dead time?

A couple of men climbed the thick willow trees and looked out over the heads of the crowd.

Now they could see him, and they shouted his name to the people below. It was Maillard. Maillard of the Bastille. Maillard of the 14th of July.

And he came forward, into the groups of people. He stopped, and managed to bring out only one word: 'Treachery!' he shouted.

Then the hurricane broke loose. 'Treachery, treachery!' Some ten men seized him and lifted him onto their shoulders. He stood aloft, steadying himself with one hand against a tree, faint from exertion, almost blinded by the sweat which trickled out of his black hair and round his eyes.

The word went forth: Maillard wants to speak. All waited, with the terrible waiting of the masses before an uprising, in the terrible seconds when the future of France was in the balance. The moment before the scale tipped, weighed down by fetters, dungeons, crosses, bibles, rosaries, crowns, sceptres, imperial orbs, bedded in the false mildness of Bourbon lilies, stuffed with hollow words and promises, screeds full of the broken oaths of kings, their unjust judgements and harmless privileges, the whole gigantic mountain of deceit inflicted on Europe over the centuries.

Maillard swung himself up into the tree.

From this bleak pulpit he cast his terrible words, over

the people, over the bare fields, over the shadowy embankments and the black drawbridges overloaded with people, into the tunnels of the city gates, over the streets of Paris, into the courtyards and the alleys of the dark quarters of the city, far far out into all the strongholds of misery, into the rat-infested underground canals everywhere where there was still a God-forsaken ear to hear him.

'To the Nation! You poor, you accursed, you outcasts! You are betrayed. You are exploited. Soon you will run about naked. You will die on the steps, and the tax farmers, Capet's henchmen, bloodhounds of the bloodhound, spiders of the spider, will wrest your last penny from your stiff fingers.

'We are deserted, we are rejected, our end is close at hand. Soon they will have snatched the last coat from our backs, and made nooses from our shirts. We will pave the filthy streets with our bodies so that the hangmen's carts can pass over. And why shouldn't we die? Our bodies poison the air, we stink, we are untouchable aren't we? Why shouldn't we die? What else is there for us to do? We can't defend ourselves, can we? They've worn us down, taken away our power of speech.

'They've created artificial price-rises, starved us out, killed us with hunger.'

Every word fell like a heavy stone into the crowd. At each syllable he threw forward his arms, as though he meant to rock the very horizon with the bombardment of his speech.

'Do you know what happened tonight?

The Queen . . .'

'Ha, the Queen.' And the masses became even quieter as they heard the hated name.

'The Queen, do you know what the old whore has done? She's brought three regiments of dragoons to Versailles. They're quartered in all the houses, and the people in the Assembly scarcely dare speak any more. Mirabeau has shrunk so small he's like a dwarf. The rest of them can hardly screw up courage to clear their throats. It's shameful to see. What use was that oath in the Jeu de Paume, if they were only playing at liberty? Why did you shed your blood at the Bastille? It was all in vain, d'you hear? In vain.

'You'll have to crawl back into your caves. The torch of freedom has become a little nightlight; a little oil-lamp. Just enough to light you back into your holes.

'In three days de Broglie will be here with his troops. The Assembly will be sent home; torture will be re-instated. The Bastille will be rebuilt, taxes will be paid. The dungeon gates are yawning open already.

'Your hunger won't be satisifed: no hope! The King stopped the bread carts before they got to Orleans and sent them home.'

His words were lost in a cry of fury. A fearful storm of clenched fists shook in the air. The masses began to well up like a tremendous maelstrom around his tree.

And the tree rose up out of the sea of cries, out of the swirling curses of distorted faces, out of a giant black whirlwind of anger which echoed down from heaven and began to shake the tree to destruction, so that it droned in the centre of the circle like the clapper of a bronze bell.

The tree rose up as though set alight by dark flames, a cold blaze shot from the abyss by a demon.

High up in its bare branches Maillard hung like a giant black bird, and wheeled his arms as though he was preparing to take flight into the evening above the mass of people, a demon of despair, a black Belial, god of the masses, throwing dark fire from his hands.

But on his forehead, flooded in unearthly whiteness by the dark light, there was reflected a golden ray, which came through the clouds, high above the chaos from the zenith of heaven.

In the west one small strip of sky had brightened; it hung over the fields like a tapestry of silken blue, still dreaming of a long silent pastoral.

Suddenly, above the storming of the masses, there twice rang out a shrill paroxysmal chorus: 'To Versailles! To Versailles!' It was as if the mass itself had uttered that cry, as if a single will had spoken what was churning in a thousand heads. Now there was a goal. The chaos was over. At a stroke, the crowd had turned into a formidable army. Their heads swung magnetically towards the western sky, where Versailles awaited them. This road they would now go down; they would wait no longer. The forces stirred up in them by the storm of despair had a will, a path. The dam was broken.

The first ranks began moving forward spontaneously, four and five abreast as the width of the road permitted.

Maillard saw it. He climbed down from his tree as fast as he could, called three men whom he knew, and ran with them over the fields alongside the column till he reached its head. There he and his men got in front of the moving tide of people and tried to persuade them to choose a leader, to fetch weapons. But no one listened to him. Now his voice was no more effective than anyone else's who might have tried to stop the iron battalions. The masses pushed him aside; the four men were no barrier to the flood which swept over them and carried them along down the road.

An invisible leader guided them, an invisible flag waved before them, a giant banner blowing in the wind, carried by a huge standard-bearer. Somebody unfurled a blood-red flag: a mighty oriflame of freedom on a purple ground which flashed ahead of them against the evening sky, red like the coming of morning.

The whole numberless crowd had become brothers, welded together by the moment of inspiration.

Men and women alike; workers, students, lawyers, white wigs, knee-stockings and sans-culottes, ladies from the Halles, fishwives, women with children in their arms, town guards swinging their pikes aloft like generals over the crowd, shoemakers with clogs and leather aprons, tailors, innkeepers, beggars and tramps, people from the suburbs, tattered and torn, an endless procession.

Bareheaded, they went on down the road. Marching songs rang out. Walking-sticks with red handkerchiefs on them were carried like standards.

Their pains were ennobled, their torture forgotten; the human being had awakened in all of them.

That was the evening when the slave, the drudge of ages, threw off his chains, and raised his head into the evening sun, a Prometheus bearing new fire in his hands.

They were weaponless. What did that matter? Leaderless. Why not? Where was their hunger and their torment now?

And the evening glow played over their faces, burning onto their foreheads a never-ending dream of greatness.

Across a mile's length of road a thousand heads burned in its light like a sea, an endless primordial sea.

Their hearts which had drowned in the murky flood of years, stifled in the ashes of drudgery, caught light on this evening glow, and began to burn again.

They held hands as they marched. They embraced. They had not suffered in vain. They all knew that the years of suffering were over, and their hearts trembled quietly.

An eternal melody filled the purple and blue of the sky; an eternal torch burned. And the sun moved before them, all the length of the evening, kindling the woods and burning the sky. And like celestial ships, manned by the spirits of freedom, great clouds sailed on the swift wind before them.

44

But the mighty poplars along the roadside blazed like great candelabra, every tree a golden flame, along the broad highroad of their glory.

The Madman

The warder gave him his things; the cashier handed him his money, the doorkeeper opened up the great iron door before him. He was in the front garden; he unlatched the garden gate and he was outside.

There. Now to show the world a thing or two.

He followed the tramlines through the low houses on the outskirts of town. He came to a field, and threw himself down among the hemlock and the thick poppy flowers at its edge. He crept right into it, like into a thick green carpet. Only his face shone out of it like a white rising moon. There. Now he was sitting, sitting!

So he was free. It was high time they'd let him out though. Otherwise, he would have killed them, the lot of them. The fat governor: he'd have got him by his pointed red beard and fed him into the sausage-making machine. Oh, what a revolting fellow he was; the way he always laughed when he passed through the butchers'.

Hell, he was a really disgusting fellow.

And the assistant doctor, that hunchbacked pig; he'd have stamped on his brains. And the warders in their white-striped aprons, who looked like a bunch of convicts; scoundrels who stole from the men and raped the women in the lavatories. It was enough to drive you mad.

He really didn't know how he'd stuck out his time there. Three or four years, how long had he actually been sitting in the depths of that white hole; that great box, surrounded by mad people. When he went to the butchers' there in the morning, across the big courtyard, how they used to lie around gnashing their teeth, a good many half naked. Then the warders came along and hauled away the ones who were acting up the worst. They were stuck in hot baths. More than one had been boiled alive, on purpose; he knew that. Once the warders wanted to bring a dead man into the butchers'. He was meant to be turned into sausages for them to eat. He told the doctor, but he talked him out of it. So the doctor must have been in league with them too, damn him. If only he had him here now. He'd throw him down in the corn and tear out his throat. That damned swine, that filthy dog, to hell with him.

And anyway, why had they brought him to the institution at all? It couldn't have been anything but spite because what else had he done? He'd knocked his wife about a bit, but he was perfectly entitled to do that; he was married to her, wasn't he? At the police station they should have thrown her out; that would have been much fairer. Instead they'd summoned him, interrogated him, made a great performance out of it. Then one morning they wouldn't let him go. They bundled him into a car and unloaded him out here. It was downright injustice, downright disgrace.

And whom had he to thank for all that? No one but his

wife. Well, now he would get even with her. She still had a lot to answer for.

In his rage he pulled a bunch of ears of corn from the edge of the field and waved it like a stick. Then he stood up, and now woe betide her.

He hoisted the pack with his things onto his shoulders and started on the march again. But he was not sure which way to go. Right in the distance, over the fields, a chimney was smoking. He knew that chimney, it wasn't far from his home.

He left the road and turned off into the fields, deep into the stalks. Straight towards his goal. What satisfaction to tread into the thick stems, making them snap and split under his feet.

He shut his eyes, and a blissful smile flitted over his face.

It seemed to him as though he was walking across a large square. Many, many people were lying there, all with their heads to the ground. It was like the picture in the governor's house where many thousands of people in white robes and hoods were lying in front of a large stone, worshipping it. And this picture was called Kaaba. 'Kaaba, Kaaba', he repeated with every step. He spoke it like a mighty incantation, and each time he trod to right and left, on the crowd of white heads. And then the skulls cracked; it sounded like someone splitting a nut with a hammer.

Some made a delicate sound, they were the thin ones; the children's skulls. It was a silvery sound, light and airy like a little cloud. But others creaked like puffballs when he trod on them, and their red tongues flickered out of their mouths, like bursting rubber balls. Oh, it was wonderfully beautiful.

Some were so soft that you sank in at once; they stuck to your feet. And so he went along with his legs in two skulls, as if he had just crept out of two egg shells which he had not yet quite shaken off.

But the thing he enjoyed most was to see an old man's head somewhere, bare and gleaming like a ball of marble. Then he positioned his foot carefully, and gave a few trial taps, like this, this, this. Then he stamped. Crack. So that the brains downright spurted, like a little golden fountain. Gradually he grew tired. He suddenly remembered the madman who believed he had glass legs and couldn't walk. He used to sit all day long on his tailor's table; but the warders always had to carry him there first. He never went a step on his own. If you stood him on his feet, he simply didn't move. Yet his legs were perfectly healthy; anyone could see that. He never even went to the lavatory on his own. How mad could you get? Quite a joke really.

The vicar had been on a visit recently, and they'd talked about the madman. 'Look, vicar, over there: the tailor. He's really off his head. What a loony!' And then the vicar had laughed so much the walls shook.

He stepped out of the corn stalks with straw all over his suit and hair. He'd lost his bundle of clothes on the way. He was still carrying the ears of corn in his hand, and he swung them before him like a golden banner. He marched straight upright, humming to himself 'Left right, left right'. And the burrs on his trousers flew off in broad arcs.

'Detachment halt!' he commanded. He stuck his banner in the sandy field path and threw himself into the ditch.

Suddenly he was afraid of the sun, which was burning his temples. He thought it was going to attack him, and he buried his face deep in the grass. Then he fell asleep.

Children's voices awakened him. Near him were standing a little boy and a little girl. When they saw the man had woken up they ran away.

A frightful rage against these two children came over him, and he went red in the face like a crab.

With one bound he sprang up and ran after the children. When they heard his footsteps they began to scream and ran faster. The small boy pulled his little sister after him. She stumbled, fell over and began to cry.

And crying was one thing he could not stand.

He caught up with the children, and pulled the little girl up out of the sand. She saw the distorted face leaning over her and screamed loudly. The boy screamed too and tried to run away. He managed to grab him with the other hand. He banged the children's heads together. One, two, three, one, two, three, he counted, and on three the two little skulls cracked together like pure thunder. Here comes the blood already! He was intoxicated; he was a god; he had to sing. A hymn came into his mind, and he sang it:

'God is a stronghold and a tower,
A help that never faileth,
A covering shield, a sword of power
When Satan's host assaileth.
In vain our crafty foe
Still strives to work us woe,
Still lurks and lies in wait
With more than earthly hate:
We will not faint nor tremble.'

He accented each beat loudly, and every time he banged the two little heads together, like a musician crashing his cymbals.

When the hymn was at an end, he let the two shattered skulls fall from his hands. He began dancing ecstatically round the two corpses. He swung his arms like a big bird, so that the blood on them scattered round him like fiery rain.

All of a sudden his mood changed. An ungovernable pity for the poor children welled up inside him and almost choked him. He lifted their bodies out of the dusty road and dragged them over into the corn. He took a bunch of weeds and wiped the blood, brains and dirt off their faces, and sat down in between the two little corpses. Then he took their little hands in his fist and stroked them with bloody fingers.

He could not help crying; big tears ran slowly down his cheeks.

It occurred to him that perhaps he could bring the children back to life. He knelt over their faces and blew into the holes in their skulls. But the children did not move. Then he thought maybe he hadn't done it long enough, and tried again. But it didn't work this time either. 'Well, can't be done,' he said. 'Dead is dead.'

Gradually countless hordes of flies, midges and other insects came out of the fields, attracted by the smell of blood. They hovered in a thick cloud over the wounds. He tried driving them off, but then he got stung himself, and decided it was too much trouble. He stood up and left. The insects descended on the bloody holes in the skulls in a black swarm.

So which way now?

Then he remembered his mission. He had to settle the score with his wife. And his face shone like a purple sun in anticipation of revenge.

He turned into a country road which led to the suburbs.

He looked around him.

The road was empty. It disappeared into the distance. Aloft on a hill behind him sat a man with a barrel-organ. Now a woman came up over the hill dragging a handcart.

He waited till she came up level with him, let her pass and then followed her.

He thought he knew her. Wasn't she the vegetable-seller from the corner? He wanted to speak to her, but he was ashamed. Oho, she'd think, that's the madman from number 17. If she recognizes me, she'll laugh in my face. I'll be damned if I'll be laughed at, I'd rather smash her skull in.

He felt the rage coming on again. He feared that dark, furious state. How vile, they'll have me back right where I came from, he thought. He felt giddy, held onto a tree and closed his eyes.

Suddenly, he saw the animal again, the one that crouched inside him, down below in his stomach, like a great hyena. What jaws the thing had. And now it wanted to be let out. Yes, yes, come on out!

Now he was himself the animal, crawling on all fours down the street. Quick, quick, or she'll run away. She can run fast! Ah, but a hyena's faster.

He barked aloud like a jackal. The woman looked round. When she saw a man running on hands and feet after her, white with dust, wild hair all over his big face, she abandoned her cart and rushed screeching down the road.

Then the animal sprang up after her like a wild thing: long mane flying, clawing the air, tongue lolling from its jaws.

Now it could hear the woman's breath. She gasped, screamed, and ran with all her might. Now! One, two, three bounds, and it's at her throat.

The woman rolls in the sand, the animal cuffs her over. Here's the throat, that's the best blood, you always drink from the throat. It sinks its jaws into her neck and sucks the blood from her body. Ugh, but that's glorious.

The animal leaves the woman lying, and springs up. There's another of them up there, coming this way. How's that for a fool? Can't he see there are hyenas round here? How can you be such an idiot?

The old man approached. When he came near he saw, through thick glasses, the woman lying in the sand with her skirts in disarray, knees drawn up to her belly in her vain fight for life. Around her head was a great pool of blood.

He stopped beside her, frozen with horror. The tall cornflowers parted and out came a man, wild and bedraggled, his mouth full of blood.

'That is certainly the murderer,' thought the old man.

In his fear he didn't rightly know what to do. Should he run or should he stay?

Finally, he decided it would be best to try friendliness, as the man wasn't quite right in the head, you could see that.

'Good day,' said the madman.

'Good day,' responded the old man. 'What a terrible accident.'

'Yes. Yes. A terrible accident, you're right there,' said the madman. His voice trembled.

'But I have to go on. Excuse me.'

And the old man went, slowly at first, then when he was a little way away, and noticed that the murderer was not following him, he went faster. Finally he began to run like a little boy.

'He certainly looks comic, running away there. What a

loony.' And the madman laughed all over his face so that the blood ran into the creases. He looked like a fiend.

Oh, let him run, why not? He's right; I'd do the same. The hyenas could come back out of the corn at any moment.

'Ugh, aren't I dirty?' He looked himself over. 'Where's all this blood come from?'

And he pulled off the woman's apron and wiped the blood off himself as best he could.

His memory faded. Finally he did not know where he was. He started out across country again, along field paths, across fields, in the burning midday. He seemed to himself like a great flower wandering through the fields. Something like a sunflower. He couldn't tell exactly.

He felt hungry.

Later, he found a turnip field, and pulled up a couple of turnips and ate them.

In one field he came across a pond.

It lay there like a big black cloth in the gold of the corn.

He felt a desire to bathe; he undressed and stepped into the water. Ah, that did you good; made you peaceful. He breathed the scent of the water; the fragrance of the wide summer fields hovered over the surface. 'Oh, water, water,' he said softly, as though calling someone. And now he swam like a big white fish in the trembling pool.

On the shore he wove himself a crown out of pond-weed and surveyed himself in the water. Then he leapt around on the shore and danced naked in the white sunlight, big, strong and handsome like a satyr.

Suddenly it occurred to him that he was doing something indecent. He dressed quickly, huddled up and crept into the corn.

If the warder comes now and finds me here, he'll give me a fine dressing-down, he'll tell on me to the governor, he thought. As nobody came, he plucked up courage and continued on his way.

All at once he found himself before a garden gate. Behind it were fruit trees. Washing had been hung upon them to dry and children were sleeping in between. He walked the length of the wall and out into the street.

There were quite a lot of people in the street, but they passed without noticing him. An electric tram went by.

He felt infinitely forlorn, overwhelmed by homesickness. For choice, he would have run right back to the institution then and there. But he did not know where he was. And who should he ask? He couldn't just go up to someone and say, 'Hey you, tell me where the lunatic asylum is.' He would certainly be taken for a lunatic, and that would not do.

And anyway, he knew very well what he wanted. There were so many things he had to settle.

At the corner of the street stood a policeman. The madman decided to ask him the way to his street, but he didn't quite dare. Finally he thought, 'I can't just stand here for ever', and started towards him. Suddenly he noticed that there was still a big bloodstain on his waistcoat. Aha! the policeman mustn't set eyes on that. And he buttoned up his overcoat. He worked out what to say, word for word, and repeated it a few times to himself.

Everything went well. He took off his hat, asked after his street, and the policeman showed him the way.

That's not far, he thought. And now he recognized the streets. Hadn't they changed, though! The trams had even got out here now.

He set off on his way, creeping along beside the houses; when he met anybody he turned his face to the wall. He was ashamed.

In this manner, he arrived at his building. There were children playing outside the door, who looked curiously at him. He climbed the stairs. There was a smell of cooking everywhere. He crept on tiptoe. When he heard a door opening below he took his shoes off as well.

Now he was in front of his door. He sat for a moment on the stairs and thought. Because this was the big moment. What had to happen, had to happen, no question.

He stood up and rang the bell. Everything remained quiet. He walked up and down the landing a few times. He read the name-plate opposite. Different people were living there now. He went back and rang again. But no one came this time either. He bent to look through the keyhole, but it was all black. He put his ear to the door to see if he could hear anything; a step perhaps, a whisper, but it was as quiet as ever.

And now a sudden thought came to him. He knew

why they weren't opening. His wife was afraid of him; she was a suspicious woman. The bitch; she knew what was up. Well, he'd see about that.

He took a few steps back. His eyes went very small, like red dots. His low forehead lowered still more. He drew himself together then sprang with a great bound against the door. It cracked, but held. He shouted at the top of his voice and sprang again. And this time the door gave. The boards split, the lock sprang loose, it opened, and he burst in.

He saw an empty flat. The kitchen was on the left, the living room on the right. The wallpaper was torn down. All over the floor was dust and peeled-off paint.

So she'd gone off and hidden herself. He ran around the four walls of the empty living-room, the little corridor, the lavatory, the bedroom. There was nothing anywhere: all empty. Nothing in the kitchen either. Then he sprang with one bound onto the stove.

And there she was, running around! She looked like a great grey rat; that was what she looked like: a rat. She kept running along the kitchen wall, round and round, and he tore an iron plate from the stove and hurled it after her. But she was too agile for him. This time I'll get her. And he threw again. This time I will. And the bombardment of iron stove rings cracked against the walls, so that the dust rustled down on all sides.

He began to shout. He bellowed as though possessed: 'You're a cow, you're a whore, you sleep with the lodgers.' It was so loud that the whole house trembled.

Doors banged all around, noise started everywhere. People on the stairs already.

Already two men standing in his doorway; behind them a crowd of women, followed by a whole battalion of small children hanging on their skirts.

The two men saw him perched on his oven, raving. They exhorted each other to be brave. A poker came flying and struck one of them on the skull; the other was felled to the ground, and with a couple of great leaps the madman bounded like a giant orang-outang across the crowd and away. He raced up the stairs, came to the attic ladder, swung himself up onto the roof, crawled over a couple of walls and around some chimneys, disappeared down a gap, rushed down some steps, and suddenly found himself in a green square. An empty bench stood in front of him. He flopped down onto it, sank his head in his hands, and began to cry softly to himself.

He needed to sleep. As he was about to stretch himself out on the bench, he saw a great crowd of people advancing down a street, with a couple of policemen leading them like generals.

'They'll be out looking for me,' he thought. 'I'm for the institution again, they think. They believe I don't have a clue what to do.'

He left the park in haste. His cap remained lying on the bench. And from a distance he glimpsed one of the men waving it in the air like a trophy.

He passed through a few crowded streets, across a square, through streets again. He began to feel uneasy among the masses of people. He felt crowded in; he looked for a quiet corner where he could lie down. One building had a palatial doorway. In front stood a man in brown livery with gold buttons. There did not seem to be anyone around but this footman. He went past him, and the man allowed him to go by without hindrance. It was rather surprising actually. Doesn't he know me, then? he wondered. And he actually felt rather insulted.

He came to a continuously rotating door. All at once, he was caught in one of the wings of this door, given a push, and suddenly found himself in a spacious hall.

There were innumerable tables, covered with lace and cloths. Everything swam in a golden light, which spread down from high windows into the twilight of the vast room. From the ceiling hung a gigantic chandelier, glittering with countless diamonds.

Great staircases ran up the side of the hall, dotted with people going up or down.

'My word, this is a fine church,' he thought. Along the aisles stood men in black suits, girls in black dresses. A woman sat behind a desk; someone was counting out money to her. A coin fell and rattled on the ground.

He went up the stairs, and through numerous great chambers full of all kinds of furniture, objects and pictures. In one of them a great many clocks were on display which all struck at once. Behind a large curtain a harmonium was playing: melancholy music which seemed to lose itself in the distance. He surreptitiously pulled back the curtain, and saw a great many people listening to a woman playing. They all looked serious and reverent, and he began to feel quite ceremonious. But he did not dare venture in.

He came to a metal latticed gate. Behind it was a deep shaft where there were some cables, apparently going up and down. A big box came up from below and the gate was drawn back. Someone said 'Going up, please.' He was in the box, and sailed aloft like a bird.

Up there he met a lot of people who were standing around big tables covered with plates, vases, glasses and jars, or moving around in the aisles between a row of stands upon which, like a field of glass flowers, there sparkled delicate crystal ware, and candlesticks and bright-coloured lamps of painted porcelain. Along the wall next to these precious things, a short staircase up, ran a narrow gallery.

He wound his way through the crowd and went up the staircase into the gallery. He leant on the balustrade, and saw the people streaming below, like countless black flies with their heads, legs and arms in endless move-ment, seeming to produce a continuous hum. And lulled by the monotony of these noises, stupefied by the sultri-ness of the afternoon, made ill by the nervous excesses of the day, he shut his eyes.

He was like a big white bird over a great lonely sea, rocked by an endless brightness, high in the blue. His head touched the white clouds, he was neighbour to the sun which filled up the sky over his head, a great golden bowl, that now began to ring with a powerful droning sound.

His pinions, whiter than a sea of snow, strong, with elbows like tree-trunks, fathomed the horizon. Below, deep in the flood, purple islands seemed to float like great rosy shells. An endless peace, an eternal rest, trembled under this eternal sky.

He did not know whether it was him flying so fast, or whether it was the sea being drawn away below him. So that must be the sea.

How envious the others would be when he told them all this tonight, in the dormitories of the institution. That was the best bit, actually. But he'd rather not tell any of it to the doctor. He'd just say 'Yes, yes' as usual, and not believe a word of it, rogue that he was. Though he always said he believed everything.

Below on the sea there floated a great white boat with slow sails. 'Like one in the Humboldt harbour,' he thought. 'Only larger.'

Goodness, but it was fine to be a bird. Why hadn't he become a bird long ago? And he rolled his arms around in the air.

Down below, a few women had become aware of him. They laughed. Others came, people began pushing and shoving, shop-girls ran for the manager.

He climbed onto the balustrade, stood upright, and seemed to be hovering over the crowd.

Below him in the ocean was an enormous light. He

62

ought to dive down, now was the time for him to sink onto the sea.

But there was something black there, something hostile; it disturbed him, it didn't want to let him go down. 'But I'll make it, of course,' he thought, 'I'm strong enough.'

He poises himself then springs from the balustrade into the middle of the Japanese glasses, the Chinese lacquer paintings, the Tiffany crystal. That's the blackness, it's here, and he pulls a shop-girl up to him, places his hands around her throat and presses.

And the people flee through the aisles, fall over each other down the stairs, shrieks fill the buildings. There's a scream of 'Fire, fire!' The whole floor is empty in the twinkling of an eye. Only two little children are left, lying in the doorway to the stairs, trampled to death, or squashed.

He kneels on his victim and slowly crushes her to death.

All around him is the great golden sea, with towering waves on either side like brilliantly shimmering roofs. He is riding on a black fish, he embraces its head with his arms. It certainly is fat, he thinks. Deep below him, he sees in the green depths, lost in a few trembling rays of sun, green castles, eternally deep green gardens. How far away might they be? If only he could just get down there, down below.

The castles go further down, the gardens appear to sink ever deeper.

He weeps; of course he's never going to get there. He's only a poor devil. The fish under him is turning disobedient too; it's still wriggling. Never mind, the beast will deal with it. And he breaks its neck.

Behind the door a man appeared, laid a gun to his cheek, aimed. The shot hit the lunatic in the back of the head. He swayed back and forth once or twice then fell heavily onto his last victim, among the clinking glasses.

And while the blood shot out of the wound, it seemed to him now as though he was sinking into the depths, ever deeper, light as a piece of down. An eternal music rose from below, and his dying heart opened, trembling with immeasurable happiness.

The Autopsy

The dead man lay alone and naked on a white table in the
big room, in the oppressive whiteness, the cruel sobriety
of the operating theatre, where the cries of endless
torments still seemed to tremble.

The midday sun covered him, and awakened the
death-spots on his forehead; it conjured a bright
green out of his naked belly and blew it up like a
big water-bag.

His body was like a giant shimmering calyx, a
mysterious plant from the Indian jungles, which someone had nervously laid at the altar of death.

Splendid red and blue colours grew along his loins,
and in the heat the big wound under his navel slowly
split like a furrow, releasing a terrible odour.

The doctors came in. Two friendly men in white coats
with duelling scars and golden pince-nez.

They approached the dead man, and looked him over
with interest, talking in scientific terms.

They took their dissecting equipment out of the white
cupboards, white boxes full of hammers, bone-saws
with strong teeth, files, gruesome batteries of forceps,
small sets of giant needles like crooked vultures' beaks
forever screaming for flesh.

They began their ghastly handiwork, looking like

fearsome torturers, with blood streaming over their hands. They delved ever deeper into the cold corpse, and brought forth its inside like white cooks disembowelling a goose.

The intestines wound around their arms, greenish-yellow snakes, and the excrement dripped onto their coats, a warm, foul fluid. They punctured the bladder; the cold urine shimmered inside like yellow wine. They poured it into large bowls; it had a sharp, biting stench like ammonia.

But the dead man slept. He patiently allowed himself to be torn at and pulled about by the hair, this way and that; he slept.

And while the hammer-blows rang down on his head, a dream awakened in him, a remnant of love which shone into his night like a torch.

Outside the big window, a great wide sky opened up, filled with little clouds swimming in light in the stillness of the afternoon, like small white gods. And the swallows circled high above in the blue, shimmering in the warm July sun.

The black blood of death ran over the blue decay of his forehead. It evaporated in the heat into a horrible cloud, and the dissolution of death crawled with its gaudy claws all over him. His skin began to fall apart. His belly grew as white as that of an eel under the greedy fingers of the doctors who dipped their arms elbow-deep in his wet flesh.

Decay pulled the dead man's mouth apart, he seemed

to be smiling; he was dreaming of a glorious star, a sweet-smelling summer evening. His decomposing lips trembled, as if touched by a fleeting kiss.

'How I love you! I have loved you so much. Shall I tell you how I love you? As you moved through the fields of poppies, yourself a flame-red fragrant poppy, the whole evening was swallowed up in you. And your dress, which billowed around your ankles, was like a wave of fire in the setting sun. But your head bent in the light, and your hair was still burning and flaming from all my kisses.

'So you went on your way, turning all the time to look at me. And the lantern swayed in your hand like a glowing rose far off into the twilight.

'I shall see you again tomorrow. Here under the chapel window, here where the candlelight falls from within, turning your hair into a golden wood, here where the narcissi brush your ankles like delicate kisses.

'I shall see you again every evening at twilight. We shall never leave each other. How I love you! Shall I tell you how I love you?'

And the dead man trembled softly with happiness on his white table, while the iron chisels in the doctors' hands broke open his temples.

Jonathan

It was the third day now that little Jonathan had been lying in the dreadful loneliness of his sickroom. The third day already, and the hours went by slower and slower. When he closed his eyes, he heard them trickling down the walls, like the continuous falling of slow drops in a dark hole in a cellar.

Since both his legs were in thick splints he could hardly move, and when the pain of his broken knees crept up on him, he had nobody to hold onto, no hand, no comfort, no gentle word. If he rang for the nurse, she came in slowly, looking surly and morose. When he complained that he was in pain, she told him she wouldn't stand for such useless grousing. That way she could be running to people a thousand times an hour, she said, and slammed the door behind her.

And then he was alone again, abandoned to his torment, a sentry at a forlorn outpost, while from above and below, and from out of the walls the pains stretched out their long white quivering fingers towards him.

The darkness of the early autumn evening crept through the empty windows into the wretched room, it grew darker and darker. Little Jonathan lay on his big white pillows, he had stopped moving. And his bed seemed to be floating down an infernal river, whose eternal cold seemed to flow into an eternally motionless waste.

The door opened, the nurse came in from the neighbouring room with a lamp. While the door was open, he caught a glimpse inside. Up till midday it had been empty. He had seen the bed, which was a huge iron one like his, standing open like a mouth ready to snap up a new patient. He could see that the bed was no longer empty. He had caught sight of a pale head lying in the shadow of the big pillow. It looked like a girl, so far as he could make out in the dim lamplight. Someone who was ill like him, a companion in suffering, a friend, someone to hold onto, someone who like him had been ejected from the garden of life. Would she answer him, what might her trouble be?

She'd seen him too; that he could tell. And their glances met in the doorway, a swift, transitory greeting, a short sign of happiness. And, like the soft wing beat of a little bird, his heart trembled with a new and mysterious hope.

Suddenly a bell rang loudly in the corridor, three bursts, sharp as a command. At the signal, the nurse ran out, shutting the door to the next room behind her.

The signal meant danger, possibly someone near to death. Jonathan had soon learnt what it meant, and he trembled with fear at the thought that someone could draw their last breath in this miserable oppressive atmosphere. Oh, why die here, where death stood, visible, at every bedside, where you were delivered up to death like a number, with seeing eyes, where every thought was infected by death, where there were no more illusions, where everything was naked, cold, and cruel. In fact a condemned man was better off, because provided he was kept in the dark about his fate, his agony only lasted one day, whereas here from the moment they came into this room they were delivered up to loneliness, to darkness, to the appalling gloom of the autumn afternoons, to winter, to death, an unending hell.

And they had to lie quietly in their beds, they had to give themselves up to physical pain, to the harrowing of their flesh. Oh, and to mock their suffering, to keep their impotence ever before their eyes, there hung on every bed-end the dying Christ on a big white cross against a darkening sky. Poor Christ; he only shrugged his shoulders sadly when the Jews begged him for a miracle; if thou art the Christ, come down from the cross. And from those fading eyes, which had already looked down on innumerable patients in these beds, from that mouth twisted in pain, which had already breathed the smell of countless horrible wounds, from everything about this crucified Thief, there emanated a fearful impotence which darkened the souls of the sick, and suffocated all that had not yet turned to death and despair.

Suddenly the door into the neighbouring room quietly opened. It had perhaps not been shut properly.

And Jonathan looked across once again into the pale face of his new neighbour, whom he had almost forgotten in his thoughts of death.

The door remained open. And the sick girl was looking over at him again, he felt it through the semi-darkness. And in these fleeting seconds they greeted each other silently across the threshold, they sized each other up, recognized each other, and joined forces like two ship-wrecked people drifting next to each other on a shoreless ocean.

'I heard you groaning so much this afternoon. Are you in a lot of pain? Why are you lying here?' he heard her say in a voice which illness seemed to have made light and delicate.

'Yes, it's awful,' said Jonathan.

'So what's the matter with you? Why did they bring you here?' she asked again.

And, in a voice quivering with pain, he told her his story.

He had set out five years ago from Hamburg, as a ship's engineer, bound for East Asia. He had knocked about the oceans of the East, always down below in the boiler-room in the seething heat of the tropics. He had been on a coral ship in the South Seas, then for over two years on a ship that smuggled opium, hidden in maize-sacks, into Canton. On that ship he made a lot of money. He wanted to go home, but then he was robbed. And there he was, naked and helpless in Shanghai. With the aid of the consul, he got a job on a ship bound for Hamburg with a cargo of rice. The ship went round the Cape to save the expense of going through the Suez Canal.

In Liberia, terrible, fever-ridden Liberia, they stopped three days in Monrovia, to take on coal. On the morning of the third day he collapsed in the stokehole. When he woke up he was lying in the public hospital, along with a hundred dirty negroes. He lay there four weeks with blackwater fever, more dead than alive. Ah! what he had to suffer there in the fearsome July heat; it burned your arteries as you lay ill, and beat into your brain like an iron hammer.

But in spite of the dirt, the stink of the negroes, the heat and the fever, it was still better than here. There they would never have been alone; they would always have been able to talk.

'Even in the midst of their fever, the negroes sang their songs and danced over their beds. And when one of them died he gave one final great bound, as if his fever were a volcano striving to hurl him once more into the air before swallowing him for ever.

'You see, I am in quarantine here, because the doctors think I might infect the others in the ward with my malaria. People like that are so careful here in Europe. They should just see how little they bother about sick people over there. But actually they get better much quicker, because they aren't shut up like criminals in this ghastly loneliness.

'My legs would heal much quicker if I wasn't so alone. But being alone like this is worse than death. Last night I woke up about three. And here I lay, like a dog on one spot, just staring into the darkness, straight ahead.'

'What have you done to your legs? May I know?' he heard her ask. 'Tell me some more.'

And he complied.

Yes, so when he was well again, he went into the Liberian jungle with a French doctor, who had set his heart on getting an orchid which was supposed to grow on the banks of the Niger. They travelled for two months through the jungle, over creeks full of alligators, across vast swamps which were so thick with mosquitoes in the evening that you could pick up hundreds of them any time you put down your hand.

And the vision of those great swamps, sinking into the jungle evening, the eternal rustling of the treetops of those limitless woods, the exotic names of strange peoples surrounded by the mystery of distance, the riddles and adventures of the remote forests, all these strange pictures filled the heart of his listener with wonder, and lifted the sick boy himself into a different atmosphere: the little ship's engineer lying on his bed of suffering in a simple, spartan hospital in Hamburg.

When he stopped talking, she begged him to continue.

And he told her the last act of his destiny, the one which had thrown him into proximity with her here, where the wide heaven of love was opening above the puritanical meanness of their two rooms, filling his heart with an undefined joy.

He emerged from the wilderness in the neighbourhood of Lagos. He joined a ship bound for home and everything went well as far as Cuxhaven. He was just going down the iron ladder to the boiler room when the ship pitched sharply in a sudden squall. He lost his balance and fell down the steps into the machinery. The piston-rods broke both his legs.

'That's too awful. That's inhuman!' said his listener, who had sat up in her pillows. Now he could see her clearly. The lamp shone on her profile. It was so pale it seemed to burn out of the darkness, like the image of a saint in a dark church.

'When I can get up, I will come and visit you. Would you like me to come and visit you sometimes?'

'Do come. Do,' he said. 'You're the first person to say a friendly word to me here. You know, if you'd come it would help me more than all the doctors. But if you're going to be up so soon, why are you here?'

She told him that she had had her appendix out, and had to stay lying here for two more weeks.

'Then perhaps we'll be able to talk more often,' said little Jonathan. 'Let's have lots more conversations.' 'Oh certainly. I'll tell the doctor; I'll ask the nurse to leave the door open for a bit again tomorrow.'

He listened, almost incredulous. And the room was suddenly empty of fear.

'Thank you.' And they both lay quiet for a while. His eyes searched for her in her pillows, and rested for a while upon her face. In the silence of these minutes his love grew deeper, it surged victoriously through his blood, it began enveloping his thoughts in happy fantasies, it showed him a broad meadow in a golden wood, it showed him a summer day, a slow summer day, a blissful noon, in which they went hand in hand through corn that whispered over their words of love.

The door opened; two doctors and two nurses came in. 'There was talking in here,' said one of the doctors. 'That won't do. It's not allowed. You must obey the hospital rules. You must have rest, do you understand? And you, nurse, see you don't leave the door open again. The patients must have quiet and be quiet.' And he went over and himself shut the door between the two rooms.

Then he examined Jonathan's legs, put on a new dressing and said, 'In three months you will perhaps be able to walk again, if all goes well. But that's still very uncertain. Meanwhile you have to get used to the idea that you may stay a cripple. I'm going to leave a nurse with you, to keep an eye on you.'

He pulled the covers back over the sick boy, wished him good-night and disappeared with his escort.

Jonathan lay in his pillows, as if someone had just torn his heart right out of his chest. The door was shut. He would never speak to her again, never be allowed to see her again. Those few moments would never come back. She would leave. In two weeks there would be someone else lying next door, some herring-merchant or some old granny. She might try once to come back but they wouldn't let her in. And in any case what would she want with a poor cripple, a legless man? The doctor had said himself that he would stay a cripple. And he sank back in despair. He lay still.

His pains came back. He clenched his teeth so as not to cry out. And the tears came into his eyes, as powerful as fire.

He shivered convulsively; he was freezing. His hands became ice-cold. He could feel the fever coming back. He wanted to call the girl's name. Then he realized that he did not know it. And this sudden recognition pushed him further into the abyss. Not even her name. He wanted to say 'Young lady!' or something like that, but as he sat up, he looked into the yellow face of his minder, which had turned old, unresponsive and mean from a thousand night-watches.

Of course, he was not alone. He had quite forgotten that. He was under guard from this Satan of a nurse, this old shrivelled devil. He was in her charge and she could boss him around. And he fell back again.

No one would save him now, no one would rescue him. And there hung Christ, that poor weakling, and continued to smile. He seemed never to be able to suffer enough, he seemed to rejoice at his torment, and Jonathan thought God's smile was strange, spiteful and false, like that of a pleasure that has been bought. He shut his eyes. He was defeated.

A raging fever took hold of him. During its initial assaults there surfaced once more in his mind, like the evening star in an empty sky, the image of his unknown neighbour; white and distant like the face of a dead person.

Towards midnight he fell asleep: the terrible paralysed

sleep that illness and despair confer on people after they have exhausted their arsenal of torments.

He slept for barely two hours. When he woke up, the pains in his thighs attacked him with such force that he almost lost consciousness. He clung with all his strength to the iron bedposts. He felt as if his legs were being pulled out with glowing tongs, and he uttered a terrible long drawn-out cry, one of those cries which so often awaken at night in hospitals, startling sleepers out of their beds, and choking every heart with fear.

He had partially raised himself in the bed. He propped himself on his hands. He held his breath with pain, sucking all the breath back into his body. And then, then: he roared out a terrible, full-throated Uuuu! Aaaa!

How Death raced through the building. He stood high up on the roof, and under his giant bony feet all the patients sat up in bed, in the big wards, in the single rooms, looking like ghosts in their white shirts by the light of the sparse lamps; and horror flew like a giant white bird across wards and stairways. The frightful roaring penetrated everywhere, waking the sleepers from their helpless sleep, arousing a terrible echo in everyone: in the cancer sufferers who had only just gone to sleep, setting the white pus running once more through their entrails; in the dying, whose bones were rotting away bit by bit; in the people with grisly sarcomas proliferating in their heads, eating away their noses, their upper jaws, their eyes, from within, drinking them up and tearing open huge stinking holes, great craters full of yellow putrid pus in their white faces.

The howling went from high to low in terrifying scales, as though directed by an invisible conductor. Sometimes there was a short interval, an artistic pause skilfully placed, until suddenly from a dark corner it began again, and swelled up until it reached the high note, a long, thin, ghastly Jiii! which floated above this sabbath of Death like the voice of a priest at mass above the singing of the choir.

All the doctors were on their feet, running to and fro between the beds, in which patients' red swollen heads stuck out like big turnips in an autumn field. All the nurses ran about the wards, white aprons fluttering, waving hypodermic syringes of morphine and boxes of opium like the ministrants of a curious religious rite.

Everywhere people were being comforted, soothed, lulled, injections of morphia and cocaine were administered to quiet the chaos; denials were issued, and encouraging bulletins given at every bedside; the wards were lighted, and with the returning light the patients' pains seemed to abate. The bellowing slowly died down to a soft whimper, and the insurrection of pain ended in tears, sleep, and resignation.

Jonathan fell into a stupor. His pain had raged itself out and was drowned in apathy.

But after the torment had left him, his legs began to swell, like two big corpses blowing up in the sun. His legs swelled up in half an hour to the size of a child's head, his feet went black and hard as stone.

When the duty doctor called on his morning rounds and lifted the covers, he saw the huge swellings under the dressing. He got an assistant to undo the bandages, cast one look at the rotting legs, then rang three times, and in a few minutes a hospital trolley was pushed in. Some men laid the patient upon it. They wheeled him out, and the room remained empty for half an hour.

Then the trolley was brought back in. On it lay little Jonathan, pale, with wide open eyes, and shorter by half. Where his legs had been, there was now a thick, bloody bundle of white cloths, which stuck out of his body like an exotic god rising from the calyx of a flower. The men threw him in the bed and left him.

He was alone for a while, and as chance would have it, in those few minutes he was able to see his acquaintance in the next-door room one more time.

The door opened again, and he again saw a white face. But it seemed like the face of a stranger, he could barely remember her. How long ago was it that he had talked with her?

She asked him how he was.

He gave her no answer, he did not hear what she asked, but he tried convulsively to pull the covers as far as possible over his bandaged leg-stumps. She must not see that below his knees there was a gap; that it was all over. He was ashamed. Shame was the only feeling he had left.

The young girl asked him again. As she once again got no answer, she turned her head away.

A nurse came in, closed the door soundlessly, and sat down with some handwork at his bed. And Jonathan fell into a restless half-sleep, stupefied by the after-effects of the anaesthetic.

Suddenly it seemed to him as if the wallpaper in the room was moving here and there. It seemed to be gently quivering in places, and swelling in and out, as if someone were standing behind it and leaning on it to tear it. And lo! all at once the wallpaper ripped at floor-level. And like a crowd of rats, armies of tiny men poured out, who soon filled up the whole room. Jonathan was surprised that so many dwarfs could have hidden behind the wallpaper. He was scandalized at such disorder in the hospital. He wanted to complain to his nurse, but when he tried to wave her to his bedside, he realized that she was not there. Now the wallpaper was suddenly all gone as well; there weren't any walls either.

He lay in a wide, huge, ward, the walls of which seemed to get further and further away until they disappeared into a leaden horizon. And the whole of this horrible desolate space was full of these little dwarfs, who were shaking their big blue heads on their narrow shoulders, like a sea of giant cornflowers on fragile stalks. Although some of them were standing quite near him, Jonathan could not recognize their faces. When he looked closely, their features dissolved into nothing but blue dots, which danced before his eyes. He would like to know how old they were, but he could no longer hear his own voice. And suddenly the thought came to him; you've gone deaf, you can't hear any more.

The dwarfs began slowly gyrating before his eyes, they moved their hands rythmically up and down; the whole mass gradually swung into movement. From right to left, right to left, his skull began to buzz. The mass whirled ever faster around him. He thought he was sitting in a great steel disk which began. turning ever faster, ever more madly around him. He grew dizzy, he wanted to hold on, but it was no good, he was carried away. He had to be sick.

Suddenly everything was still, empty, gone. He lay alone and naked in a large field on a sort of bier.

It was very cold, with a storm blowing up; in the sky a black cloud moved upwards, like a giant ship with black swelling sails.

In the distance at the edge of the sky stood a man, wrapped in a piece of grey cloth, and although he was far away, Jonathan knew exactly who he was. He was bald, with very deep-set eyes. Or perhaps he had no eyes?

On the other side of the sky he saw a woman standing, or a young girl. She looked familiar, he had seen her before, but a long time ago. Suddenly the two figures began beckoning to him, waving their long wrinkled sleeves; but he did not know which to obey. When the girl saw that he made no move to come down from his bier she turned round and moved off. He saw her walking away for a long time against the white-streaked sky.

Finally, when she was far off, right in the distance, she stopped once more. She turned round and waved to him once more. But he could not stand up, he knew; terrifying old Death's Head out there wouldn't allow it. And the girl vanished into the lonely sky. But the man beckoned him ever more strongly, threatening him with his bony fist. Then, he crawled down from his bier, and dragged himself over the fields, over deserts, and all the time the apparition flew ahead of him, ever further through darkness, through terrible darkness.

The Ship

It was a small boat, carrying coral, which cruised the Arafura Sea by way of Cape York. Sometimes they saw the mountains of New Guinea ahead of them in the blue north; sometimes in the south the bare Australian coastline, lying like a dirty silver girdle across the shimmering horizon.

There were seven men on board. The captain, an Englishman, two other Englishmen, an Irishman, two Portuguese and the Chinese cook. And because they were so few, they had remained good friends.

Now the ship was going down to Brisbane. There they were to unload and the men would split up and go their separate ways.

On their way they sailed through a little archipelago, a few islands to the right and left, remains of the great bridge that once, an eternity ago, joined the two continents of Australia and New Guinea. Now the ocean roared over it, and the plumbline took ages to hit bottom.

They ran the boat into a little shady harbour and dropped anchor. Three men went ashore to look for the inhabitants of the island.

They waded through the shoreline woods, struggled up and down a mountain, traversed a ravine, then another wooded mountain. And after a few hours they came again to the sea. Nowhere on the island was there a single living thing. They heard no birdsong, no animal crossed their path. Everywhere there was an awful silence. Even the sea ahead of them was grey and dumb. 'But there must be someone here, God damn it,' said the Irishman.

They called, they shouted, they fired off their revolvers. Nothing moved, nobody came. They wandered along the beach, through water, over rocks and through shoreline bushes; they met nobody. The tall trees looked down on them without rustling, like great ghostly beings, huge corpses, stiffened into ghastly immobility. A feeling of oppression came over them, sombre, mysterious. They wanted to talk each other out of their fear. But when they looked into each other's white faces, they remained silent.

They finally came out onto a tongue of land, the last projection of the island jutting into the sea like a final point of retreat. At the outermost tip, where their path turned back, they saw something which stopped them in their tracks.

There lay, tangled together, and still in their primitive underclothes, the corpses of two men and a woman. They were covered all over, on their breasts, arms and faces, with red and blue spots like thousands of insect bites. And a few large boils had erupted here and there, like hills, out of their splitting skins.

They left the bodies as fast as they could. It was not

death that made them run. But an unexplained menace seemed printed on the faces of these corpses; something bad seemed to lurk, invisible, in the still air, something for which they had no name but which was undeniably there, an inexorable icy fear.

Suddenly they began to run, tearing themselves on the thorns. Ever farther. They practically trod on each other's heels.

The last one, an Englishman, got caught on a bush and, as he tried to free himself, he happened to look round. And he thought he saw something behind a great tree-trunk, a small black figure like a woman in mourning.

He called his comrades and pointed to the tree. But there was nothing there now. They laughed at him, but their laughs rang hoarse.

At last they got back to the ship. The boat was launched and brought them on board.

As if by a secret accord, they said nothing about what they had seen. Something sealed their lips.

When the Frenchman was leaning on the rails that evening, he looked down and saw that the rats were leaving the ship in droves, swarming out of the hull from every nook and cranny. Their fat brown bodies were swimming everywhere in the waters of the bay; the water was glistening with them.

Without any doubt, the rats were moving out.

He went to the Irishman and told him what he had seen. But he was sitting on a rope, staring straight ahead of him and would not listen. He went to the Englishman in front of the cabin, but he stared at him so furiously that he went away.

Night fell, and the crew went down to their hammocks. All five men slept together. Only the captain slept alone, in a cabin towards the stern, under the deck. And the Chinaman's hammock hung in the galley.

When the Frenchman came down from the deck, he saw that the Irishman and the Englishman had got into a fight. They reeled around among the ship's boxes, their faces blue with fury. And the others stood round and watched. He asked one of the Portuguese why the two had come to blows, and was told it was over a length of wool for darning socks which the Englishman had taken off the Irishman.

Finally they gave up, and each crept into a corner of the cabin and sat unresponding as the others jeered at them.

Finally, all lay in their hammocks; only the Irishman rolled his up and took it on deck.

The hammock could be seen above them through the cabin door, like a black shadow, slung between the bowsprit and a rope, swaying to and fro with the gentle rocking of the ship.

And the leaden atmosphere of a tropical night, full of heavy mists and sticky vapours, sank over the ship, and covered it in a sinister, comfortless veil.

Everyone was already asleep, lying terribly still, and their breathing sounded into the distance with a muffled one, as though from under the heavy lid of a giant black coffin.

The Frenchman struggled against sleep, in vain. He felt himself giving in, and the first wavering dream-images passed before his closing eyes, forerunners of sleep. A little horse, then some men with enormous old-fashioned hats, then a fat Dutchman with a long white misty beard, then some little children, and behind them something that looked like a big hearse advanced through hollow alleys in a gloomy half-darkness.

He fell asleep. And in the last moment he had the feeling that someone was standing in the corner, staring fixedly at him. He wanted to force open his eyes once more, but a leaden hand closed them.

And the long swell undulated under the black ship; the wall of jungle threw its shadow into the barely illuminated night, and the ship sank deep into the midnight darkness.

The moon stuck up its golden skull between two tall palms. For a short while it was light, then the moon disappeared in thick, drifting mist. It reappeared only occasionally, in between moving wraiths of cloud, small and murky, like the terrible eye of a blind man.

Suddenly a long cry tore the night, sharp as an axe.

It came from the captain's berth astern, as loud as if it had been uttered directly next the sleeping men. They started up in their hammocks, and in the half-darkness looked into each other's white faces.

There was a few seconds' silence; then suddenly it rang

out again three times, very loud. And the screaming awakened a fearful echo in the depths of the night, somewhere in the rocks, and again, very distant now like a laugh dying away.

The men groped around for light, but could not find any. They crawled back into their hammocks and sat bolt upright in them, speechless, as though paralysed.

And after a few minutes they heard a dragging step coming over the deck. Now it was over their heads, now a shadow passed the cabin door. Now it went towards the bows. And while they stared at each other with wide-open eyes there came, from the hammock of the Irishman, another loud, long drawn-out death wail. Then a rattle, very, very short, a trembling echo and then the stillness of the grave.

And suddenly the face of the moon, big and white like a fat Malay's, pushed into their doorway, crossed the steps, and mirrored itself in their ghastly pallor.

Their taut lips gaped, and their jaws vibrated with fear.

One of the Englishmen made a single attempt to speak, but his tongue curled back onto itself in his mouth, then fell out suddenly like a red rag over his lower lip. He was paralysed, and could not withdraw it.

Their foreheads were chalk-white, beaded with the cold sweat of extreme terror.

And so the night passed, in the fantastic half-darkness that the big sinking moon cast upon the cabin floor. But curious signs like ancient hieroglyphics kept appearing on the sailors' hands: triangles, pentagrams, drawings of skeletons, deaths' heads with big bat-wings growing out of their ears.

Slowly the moon sank. And at the moment when its gigantic head dropped out of sight behind the companionway, they heard a dry groan coming from the galley aft, and then, quite clearly, a soft cackle like an old person's laugh.

And the first grey of morning flew with ghastly wings over the sky.

They looked in each other's ashen faces, climbed out of their hammocks, and crawled up on deck with shaking limbs.

The paralysed man with the hanging-out tongue came up last. He wanted to say something, but could bring out nothing but a gruesome stammer. He pointed to his tongue and made pushing-back movements. And one of the Portuguese seized the tongue with fingers that were blue with fright, and forced it back into his gullet.

They stayed huddled together in the hatchway, and anxiously scanned the gradually lightening deck. But there was no one there. There was only the Irishman in the bows swinging to and fro in his hammock in the fresh morning wind like a giant black sausage.

And all together they advanced slowly on the sleeper as if magnetized, shaking in every limb. Nobody called to him, everyone knew that there would be no answer. Everyone wanted to postpone the gruesome revelation as long as possible. And now they were there, and craned their necks to stare at the black bundle in the hammock.

His woollen blanket was pulled up to his forehead. And his hair fluttered down over his temples. But that hair was no longer black; in the night it had gone snow-white. One of them pulled the blanket off his head, and they saw the pallid face of a corpse, staring up at the sky with wide-open, glazed eyes. The forehead and the temples were strewn with red blotches, and a big black boil swelled out at the root of his nose like a horn.

'It's the plague.' Which of them had spoken? They looked aggressively at each other and then quickly backed out of the lethal presence of the dead man.

Suddenly they all realized together that they were doomed. They were in the pitiless hands of a terrible invisible enemy who was perhaps only gone for a short while. Any moment he could step down from among the sails; this very second he could come out of the cabin, or rear his terrible face over the side and pursue them wildly round the deck.

And in each of them, for no reason he could explain, there grew a lowering resentment against his companions in misfortune.

They moved apart. One positioned himself next to the ship's boat, his pale face mirrored in the water below. The others sat down anywhere on the bench round the side, not speaking, but near enough each other to be able to run together again immediately, should the danger become tangible. But nothing happened. And yet they all knew that it was there, lying in wait for them.

90

It was lurking somewhere. Perhaps in the very midst of them on the deck like an invisible white dragon reaching for their hearts with its quivering fingers and spreading the poison of sickness with its warm breath.

Weren't they ill already, didn't they feel a kind of heavy lethargy, the sense of a deadly fever coming on? The man by the rail felt as though the ship was beginning to rock and sway, now quickly, now slowly. He looked around for the others and saw nothing but greenish faces in the shadows, their sunken cheeks already scattered with frightening blotches of livid grey.

'Perhaps they're already dead, and I'm the only one left alive,' he thought. And fear ran ice-cold all over his body. It was as though an icy hand had reached out of the air and grabbed him.

Slowly day came.

Over the grey plains of sea, over the islands, over everywhere, lay a grey mist, damp, warm and suffocating. At the edge of the ocean was a little red dot, like an inflamed eye. The sun was rising.

And the torment of waiting for the unknown drove the men from their places.

What now? They had to go down below sometime, eat something.

But then came the thought: perhaps they'd have to walk over dead bodies.

There! They heard a muffled bark on the stairway. The ship's dog poked out its muzzle, then began to emerge backwards; the body, finally the head; but what was that hanging from its mouth? A hoarse cry of horror broke from all four throats.

From its mouth hung the body of the old captain; first his hair, then his face, then his whole fat body in a dirty nightshirt came out, slowly dragged onto the deck by the dog. And now he lay outside, by the cabin stairs, with the same dreadful red patches burning on his face.

The dog let go of him and slunk away.

Suddenly they heard him growling loudly in a distant corner. He came bounding forward again from the stern of the ship, but by the mainmast he stopped still, whirled around, and stretched his legs in the air as though defending himself against an unseen tormentor whose merciless claws never relaxed their grip.

The dog's eyes started out as though they were on stalks; his tongue came out of his mouth. There was a rattle in his throat as though he was being strangled. He was shaken by a last convulsion, stretched out his legs and died.

And immediately afterwards the Frenchman heard the dragging step near him quite clearly, and horror beat upon his skull like a hammer of bronze.

He wanted to shut his eyes but could not; he was no longer master of his own will.

The steps advanced straight across the deck, towards the Portuguese, who was leaning backwards against the hull of the ship, his hands clawing madly at the ship's side.

The man could obviously see something. He wanted

to run away, he appeared to be trying to tear his legs from the ground, but he had no strength. The invisible being seemed to grab him. With the utmost exertion, he wrenched his teeth apart, and stammered in a metallic voice that seemed to come from very far away: 'Mother, mother.' His eyes wandered, his face turned ashen, his taut limbs sagged. He keeled over, and his forehead hit the deck.

The invisible being continued on its way; he heard the dragging steps again. It seemed to be heading for the two Englishmen. And the same dreadful scene was enacted again. The same word was forced twice from their throats by the ultimate fear: 'Mother, mother.' And on that cry they died.

'And now it will come to me,' thought the Frenchman. But it did not come. All remained still. And he was alone with the dead.

The morning went by. He did not move from the spot. He had only one thought: when would it come? His lips kept mechanically repeating the one little sentence: 'When will it come? When will it come?'

The mist had gradually dispersed. And the sun, which was already near noon, had changed the sea into an enormous shining expanse, a gigantic silver dish beaming its light into space like a second sun.

It was quiet again. The atmosphere simmered with tropical heat. The very air seemed to be boiling. And the sweat ran in thick furrows over his grey face. The sun beat upon his crown, and his head felt like a giant red tower full of fire. He saw his head quite clearly from inside growing up into the sky. Ever taller and ever hotter he grew within. But inside something was crawling, very slowly, up a winding staircase whose last spirals disappeared into the white fire of the sun. It was a slippery white snail. Its antennae were feeling their way up the tower, while its wet tail was still twisting in his neck.

He had a dark feeling that it had become simply too hot, that no one could stand that heat.

Then — bang! — someone hit him on the head with a fiery staff, and laid him out full length. This is death, he thought. And now he lay for a while on the burning-hot ship's planks.

Suddenly he woke up again. A sound of soft reedy laughter was fading away behind him. He looked up and saw that the ship was moving, it was moving, and all the sails were full. They bellied out, white and billowing, but no wind was stirring, not the slightest breath. The sea lay as bright as a mirror: white, a fiery hell. And high up in the sky the sun at its zenith was liquefying like a giant mass of white-hot iron. It bombarded the sky with fire, adhering to what it struck so that the very air seemed to burn. Right in the distance like a scattering of blue dots lay the islands where they had anchored.

And all of a sudden the horror surfaced again, like a gigantic millipede swarming through his arteries and freezing them stiff at the touch of its myriad cold legs.

Before him lay the dead men. But now they were face-up. Who had turned them over? Their skin was blueish green. Their white eyes stared at him. Incipient decay had drawn their lips apart and puckered their cheeks into a demented smile. Only the corpse of the Irishman slept peacefully in his hammock. He tried very slowly pulling himself up on the side of the ship, his mind a blank.

But the unspeakable fear made him weak and powerless. He sank to his knees. And now he knew; now it would come. Something was standing behind the mainmast. A black shadow. Now it came over the deck with its dragging step. Now it stood behind the roof of the cabin; now it came out. An old woman in a black dress of antiquated style; long white locks falling on either side of her pale old face, in which stuck two eyes of nondescript colour like buttons that stared unblinking at him. Her face was scattered all over with the blue and red pustules, crowned upon the forehead by two red boils, partly covered by her white grandmother's cap. Her black crinoline rustled as she came towards him. With a last despairing effort he dragged himself upright by his hands and feet. His heart stopped. He fell back again.

And now she was so near that he could see her breath blowing out of her mouth like a banner.

He righted himself once again. His left arm was already paralysed. Something forced him to stay still, something gigantic held him fast. But he still didn't give up the struggle. He pushed the something down with his right hand, he tore himself free.

And with swaying steps, he hurried recklessly along the side, past the dead man in the hammock, to the bows, where the big rope ladder ran up from the end of the bowsprit to the foremast.

He climbed up it; he looked around.

But the plague was after him. She was already on the lowest rungs. So he had to go higher, higher. But the plague kept on coming, she was faster than him, she was bound to catch him up. He gripped the ropes with hands and feet at random, put one foot right through the mesh, pulled it out again, arrived at the top. The plague was still a few yards away. He climbed along the yard at the top. There was a rope at the end of it. He came to the end of the yard. But where was the rope? There was nothing but space.

Far below was the sea and the deck. And directly below him lay the two dead men.

He wanted to go back, but the plague was already at the end of the yard.

And now she was advancing unsupported along the wooden bar, with the rolling gait of an old sea dog.

Now it was only six steps to go; now only five. He counted each of them under his breath, and the fear of death stretched open his jaws in a convulsive movement like a great yawn. Three steps. Two steps.

He retreated, grasped at the air, tried to get a hold somewhere, tipped over and dived head first with a crash onto an iron plank in the deck. And there he lay, his skull shattered.

A black storm blew up quickly in the east over the quiet ocean. The sun hid in the black clouds, like a dying person pulling the sheet over his face. A couple of big Chinese junks which had sailed up in the half darkness had put out all their sails and were running tumultuously before the storm, with prayer-lamps burning and pipes playing. But the ship passed in front of them, supernaturally large like the flying shadow of a demon. On the deck stood a black figure. And in the fiery light it seemed to grow, and its head towered slowly over the masts, while its mighty arms circled like a crane flying into the wind. A wan-coloured hole opened up in the clouds. And the ship sailed straight into the terrible brightness.

An Afternoon

Contribution to the History of a Little Boy

The street looked to him like a long pencil-stroke, with passers-by who were no more than inflated white dolls. They couldn't know about his happiness, could they? He had asked her, 'May I kiss you?', this little boy, and she had held out her lips and he had kissed them. And this kiss burnt deeply into his heart, like a big pure flame, which released him, made him happy, made him blissful. Ye Gods, he would like to have danced with happiness. And the sky ran away above him like a great blue road; the light travelled westwards like a fiery waggon, and all the glowing houses seemed to reflect the blaze.

He felt as if his life were thunderously large, as though he had never lived so much before, as if he were swimming high in the air like a bird, sunk in the eternal ether, boundlessly free, boundlessly happy, boundlessly alone.

And the invisible crown of happiness lay on his square childish forehead and beautified it, like a night landscape lit by multiple flashes of lightning.

'Ye Gods! I'm loved! I'm loved! What it is to be loved so much!' He went faster, broke into a run, as though his usual measured gait were too slow for the storm rushing in his heart. In this state he ran down the street and sat by the sea.

'Oh sea, sea!' and he told his experience to the sea, in a brief shout of joy, a trembling whisper, a flurry of silent speech. And the sea understood him and listened to him, the sea, over whose blue droning expanse the hurricane of joy and the sobs of grief had reverberated for so many millennia, like a perpetual whirlwind over an eternally untouched deep.

He preserved his loneliness nervously. When people came he sprang up, ran away and crept into the dunes. Once they had gone by, he ran forward again to the sea, whose enormous expanse was the only cup into which he could pour the flood of his endless excess.

Gradually the beach grew livelier. White dresses were flashing all over the place between the basket-chairs, old ladies came with books under their arms. Bright sun-shades bobbed on the narrow wooden walkways, and crowds of children filled up the sand-castles again. Rowing-boats put out to sea, sails were hoisted on the big yachts, a photographer waded through the sand with his camera on a strap over his shoulder.

He looked at the time. A half an hour more, twenty-nine minutes, then he'll be meeting her. He will take her by the hand, they will go together into the wood, where it's perfectly quiet. And there they will sit down together, hand in hand, hidden in the green thicket.

But what will he say, to stop her thinking he's boring? Because she's like a little lady already, you have to entertain her, make jokes.

Whatever should he say to her?

Oh, he won't speak at all, and she'll understand him that way too. They will look into each other's eyes, and their eyes will say quite enough.

And then she will hold out her mouth to him again, he will take her head lightly in his arm, like this, like this – he tried it on a stalk of broom – and then he will kiss her, very softly, very tenderly.

And they will sit that way, together in the wood, together until dark; oh how lovely, how lovely, what complete bliss.

They will never leave each other. He will work all the time, he will get through his studies quickly, and one day he will marry her. And life seemed to the child like a clear straight road, leading into a sky of endless blue, short, simple, uneventful, like an endless garden.

He stood up and went over the beach through the playing children, the people, and the basket-chairs. A steamer came in, a stream of people swelled towards the landing-stage. A bell was rung. He saw none of it; the things which would previously have riveted his attention had disappeared. His eyes were directed inwards, as though he needed all his time to study the new person that had suddenly emerged from the locked core of his being.

He came to the bench where he was to meet his little girlfriend; she was not yet there.

But of course it was still too early. There were still ten minutes to go. She probably had to have coffee before leaving; her mother wouldn't have let her go yet.

He sat for a few minutes on the bench, then stood up again and ran back and forth a few times in the little circle of trees. Only two minutes left, he should be able to see her by now. He scanned the path for her. But the path stayed empty. Its trees hid nobody. They stood, softly gilded by the afternoon sun, peaceful in the windless air, and through their foliage the light trembled on the path, like on the bed of a golden stream. The tree-lined walk was like a great, green, quiet hall, with a doorway at the far end, in which there shimmered a small blue stripe, the distant meeting-point of sea and sky.

He trembled. Something contracted inside him. 'Why doesn't she come? Why doesn't she come?'

'Ah, isn't that her hat, isn't that the white ribbon? That's her, that's her.'

And the door of his soul sprang open, he was shaken by a storm, he ran to meet her. As he came nearer, he saw that he had made a mistake. That wasn't her at all, it was someone else. And that moment he felt something being stifled in him, as though he was being strangled.

He had a familiar feeling suddenly: like once when they were taking him out of a house where there was a dead person and he had stood by the bedside: a sort of disgust, or self-loathing. This particular, strange feeling always came over him when something unpleasant was approaching which he could not get out of; mathematics homework, a telling-off.

But he had never felt it so strongly before. He could almost taste it on his tongue, bitter, like something grey.

His blood seemed to stand still; it was uncanny to be so inert. His forehead had gone small, and grey, as though someone had overshadowed it with their hand.

He went back slowly to the circle under the tree. 'But she'll come, of course she will.' Of course she could be late. If only she would come! She could be a quarter of an hour late as far as he was concerned, just so long as she finally came.

He looked at his watch again. The time had gone by, and the second hand ran ever further ahead like a small thin spider in a silver cage. Its little foot trod on the seconds, which fell away in little jerks, like dust on a tiny country road.

Now four minutes had gone by already, now five. And the minute hand climbed even higher up its little stair. He wanted to go and meet her. But what if she came from another direction? He hesitated; should he stay, should he go? But his unrest drove him out. He ran back a few steps down the path, then he stopped again, and again turned back.

He sat down on the bench, and stared ahead of him. And with every minute his confidence diminished. He would wait till five o'clock; she could still come.

From the distance you might have taken him for an old man from the way he was sitting. Bent, sunk into himself like someone over whom many years of grief have rolled.

He stood up again, and went slowly a few more steps over the scene of his childish tragedy.

In the distance he heard a clock striking, but it was fast. He compared it with his pocket watch. That one was certainly striking too soon. There were still three minutes to five.

And in these three minutes hope reared up once again in his heart: a feeling of longing, like the dying flame from a sinking ember, or like the salute to life in the last heartbeat of a dying person.

Now, now it was time. Now all the towers in the town behind the wood were striking. He saw a bell swinging in the clear air, up in the belfry of a church tower. And at every droning stroke, he felt that his heart was being tugged out of his breast, a little way at a time to make the pain last longer. One tug, another, soon it will be right out, he thought.

The towers went silent; it was quiet again. And in his breast it went quite empty, it was as if there were a great empty hole, as though he were carrying around a dead thing inside.

It felt as though something stupefying had been poured into his blood. It made his head so heavy, it made him so tired.

Over a sunny pond that shimmered through the trees of the public gardens a few puffs of cloud emerged from the chimney of the swimming baths. They flew away in the wind. He watched without interest as they dissolved in the light. Two voices became audible behind the bushes. A pair of nursemaids came along pushing prams.

They settled opposite him on the bench in the circle and lifted the children out of the prams, who straightaway tumbled down a heap of sand.

Then he stood up and went away, slowly, his mind a blank.

He came down onto the beach again. He went through the basket-chairs again. The old ladies were still sitting there with their books, the photographer was there, standing in front of a group of people. He must have made a joke, for all of them had laughing faces.

He was carried by the force of his passion towards the basket-chair in which he had received the kiss at midday, like a little ship driven pitilessly by the storm towards a rock.

Perhaps she was still sitting in it. That was his last hope. He slid cautiously between the basket-chairs, nearer and nearer. And the red pennant on top seemed to wave to him.

Now he was very near. He was halted by a vague fear. Then he heard her voice. She was laughing. And now another voice: a boy's.

He crept warily forwards, taking a circuitous route. He dropped into the sand and advanced on all fours. When he was near enough to see them he lay down behind a heap of sand and raised his head slightly over the top.

She was sitting on a boy's lap. The boy pulled her head down to kiss her, then as he released it his hand reached for her leg. The hand slid upwards slowly, and she leaned back, right back, against his shoulder.

The little boy withdrew his head and crept away, putting one leg behind the other, one hand behind the other, mechanically.

He didn't actually feel anything, no pain, no anguish. He had just one wish, to hide, to creep in somewhere and then lie quite still, find himself a little spot somewhere in the lyme-grass.

And when he was far enough away, he got up out of the sand and went.

On the way he saw a schoolfriend, and hid from him behind a tent. His mother came from the right and called him over. He behaved as though he hadn't heard anything. He began to run, past the basket-chairs, past the people. And as he ran it occurred to him that he had run like this already today, at midday when he was so happy.

Then he was overcome by grief. He got away quickly up the dunes. At the top he threw himself down with his face in the stalks. The lyme-grass nodded over his head like a wood; a pair of dragonflies hummed through the stalks.

And that was the first time in the boy's life that he drank the cups of rapture and of torment in the same day. So many times afterwards it was to be his lot to suffer the extremes of joy and the depths of grief, like a precious vessel that has to be able to withstand many passages through the fire without cracking.